Ransack - Text copyright © Emmy Ellis 2023
Cover Art by Emmy Ellis @ studioenp.com © 2023

All Rights Reserved

Ransack is a work of fiction. All characters, places, and events are from the author's imagination. Any resemblance to persons, living or dead, events or places is purely coincidental.

The author respectfully recognises the use of any and all trademarks.

With the exception of quotes used in reviews, this book may not be reproduced or used in whole or in part by any means existing without written permission from the author.

Warning: The unauthorised reproduction or distribution of this copyrighted work is illegal. No part of this book may be scanned, uploaded, or distributed via the Internet or any other means, electronic or print, without the author's written permission.

RANSACK

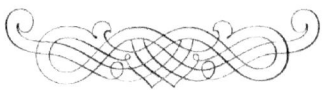

Emmy Ellis

Chapter One

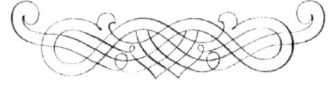

Lillibet moved her finger from the nine on her phone keypad and prodded CONTACTS. She wouldn't get hold of the police. Instead, she selected DEBBIE and pressed the icon. Held her breath as it rang. A killer was out there, targeting working girls, and Lillibet reckoned she'd just seen him. A balaclava hiding his identity, he'd been at her front door, posting a note—and he was coming for her.

Debbie answered on the seventh ring—she must have been occupied, as she normally responded faster than that, seeing as she was Lillibet's boss. "I thought this was your night off, madam?"

"There was a man here. That bloody killer," Lillibet blurted.

"*What?*"

"He… I was at the Plaza, the casino, and I came out to get a taxi." She wouldn't tell Debbie she'd contemplated walking home in the dark, she'd get told off. "He stopped, must have thought I was working—he might already have *known* I'm a sex worker. *And* he knows my name. Oh God…what if he's been watching me?"

"Take a deep breath, love, then tell me what happened next."

"Okay. I shook my head at him, and he drove off on that long road that leads to my place. But he parked halfway down, like he was waiting to see what I'd do next. I got in my cab, went indoors, and the next thing I knew, he was outside. He had a balaclava on and posted a note through my bloody door."

"Jesus. Are you okay?"

"Of course I'm not!"

Debbie tutted. "I meant, did he harm you?"

"No. He's gone now. I rang you straight away. The note shit me up."

"What did it say?"

"*Hello, Lillibet. You're next.*"

"Christ. Has he's really gone?"

"Yes."

"Right, make sure you're locked in. I'm coming round for you. Stay on the line, on speaker. Pack a bag, because you're not staying there on your own. You need to be somewhere else until this fucker is caught."

Lillibet jabbed the speaker icon and popped her phone between her bra cups. She walked around the house, checking windows and the exit doors, letting Debbie know the status along the way. Everything was secure, so she got on with putting some clothes in a suitcase. She lugged it downstairs, jumping at the flash of headlights coming through the mottled glass in the front door.

"I'm here," Debbie said, her voice muffled by Lillibet's boobs.

Lillibet opened the front door and, as she still had her coat and shoes on from when she'd arrived home, she went out onto the path. She stared ahead, up the road that led to the Plaza. No red taillights, so he'd definitely gone. Unless he'd parked between lampposts, turned his engine off, and she couldn't see his car. She switched her attention to the one parked at the kerb, the window down, Debbie's face peering out at her. Relief smacked into Lillibet that she'd be safe now, and she closed the door, dragging her case down the path. She put it on the back seat and got in the passenger side.

"Did you bring the note?" Debbie asked. "The Brothers are going to want to see it."

"Shit." Lillibet dashed back inside, collected it, and returned to sit next to Debbie. She popped the note in her handbag. "Get me out of here, for fuck's sake."

Debbie drove away, her window sailing back up. "You must be so scared."

"That's an understatement. He knows my name, knows where I live, which means he's been *watching* me."

"And he must have been watching the ones he's already killed, which explains why none of the girls have been murdered while at work—he got them on their days off."

"But he thought *I* was working tonight. I told you, he stopped, the window going down a bit so all I saw were his eyes. What was he going to do, take me off in his car and murder me? Sounds like it. So the other women weren't working either. Did he approach them and they decided, fuck it, I'll earn a bit of extra money?"

"I think it's time for me to call a meeting with all the girls from the parlour, my corner, and Kitchen Street. We need to have a proper plan, not just my previous message telling them to be careful. Yes, I provide taxis after work, but that doesn't keep everyone safe when they're not doing a shift."

"He's killed three so far. Why haven't the police caught him yet?"

"They never caught Jack the Ripper…"

Unease slithered through Lillibet. The thought that the man had targeted women—and *her*—when they'd had no idea they were being observed brought home how vulnerable they were in the profession they'd chosen. She used to work at Ford and Sons during the day, but overspending had forced her to find more work to pay off her debts, and she'd met Crook, her old pimp. He was 'missing' now, courtesy of The Brothers, and Debbie had taken over his patch at Kitchen Street, employing Lillibet and Sharny Baker as street managers. They still went with punters, but they also got paid for being there for the other women and reporting anything iffy. Lillibet worked during the day, and she made so much money she'd given up her job with Mr Ford.

It was just as well, distancing herself from that place. It was where she'd met Fiona, Theresa, Pippa, and Stephanie. Where her life had changed forever. Stephanie had pissed them off, and they'd gone round to hers to beat her up. Except the beating had turned fatal, and Stephanie had died from their kicks to her head. Pippa had moved up north, Fiona had left Fords', but Theresa was still there, climbing the ladder. They'd promised to keep it a secret that they'd collectively killed someone, and Lillibet had no intention of ever confessing, but she worried the others might crack one day.

She stared through the windscreen. "Have The Brothers already been trying to find the killer?"

Debbie nodded. "Yes, but whoever it is, he doesn't want to be found, and he's clever. We've already had a chat about ensuring you're all safe, obviously, and I think it helps because we have watchers keeping an eye on you all, plus the screening system so all customers are in our database. The killer may have tried to get one of the girls to go with him, and when he was told his name needed to be checked, he drove away. That's not unusual, so none of you would have batted an eyelid at that. Some men don't want to give their names—they're married or whatever and worry about their missus finding out what they're up to."

Lillibet remembered something. "I have his number plate. I memorised it and put it in my notes app."

"Brilliant. The twins' copper will be able to look that up, seeing as she's on the killer case. Did you see the news earlier? They're calling him the Slasher now."

Lillibet shivered. All the dead women had been cut. The news outlets were having a field day with this, ramping up the fear, and one channel reported on it all day, repeating the same stuff over and over. Lillibet usually caught up on it when she got home from work, but she *did* check her phone in quiet times in the hope they'd caught him and they could all relax.

"He'll be on the prowl now," Lillibet said. "What if he goes for someone else tonight?"

"But the note said you're next."

"I know, but what if he's got the urge and can't control it? Some poor cow could be being sliced up right this second."

Debbie pulled into the car park beside her pub, The Angel. She switched the engine off, and the darkness gave Lillibet the willies, especially as the cemetery was off in the distance ahead. While she couldn't see it, she knew it was there. Those places had always given her the creeps.

"Look," Debbie said, "if you're next and he sticks to a rigid plan, that's a good thing. It means no one will be killed until he finds you—which he won't. It'll give the twins time to up their search and stop him."

"But what if he didn't mean I'm next specifically, just that I'm next at some point? He could have a list of us that he chooses from. And how the fuck does he know my name and where I live?"

"He could be a customer, could even be in our database. Think about it, if he poses as being a regular, handing his name over without any fuss, no one would suspect him. I'll put that to George and Greg, because as far as I know, they haven't gone through our list of punters yet, but I could be wrong there. Come on, let's get you inside."

Debbie took charge of the suitcase and led the way up steel steps attached to the side of the pub, the security light snapping on. She ushered Lillibet in and closed the door. "Wait there until I've checked the flat."

Lillibet's heart pounded. "What, you think he might be *here*?"

"No, I always check the place, even though my exit doors are steel. Habit."

Lillibet remained by the door with her case. Debbie stalked off in the darkness, then lights flashed on farther down the hallway. She came out of a side door and walked across into another room calling, "All clear."

Lillibet followed her, going into a kitchen.

Debbie faffed about with a Tassimo machine, put a cup beneath the spout, and pressed a button. "Right, I'll ring the twins now." She left.

Lillibet swallowed. She'd seen them around, they regularly passed by on Kitchen Street, likely making sure everything was okay, but she hadn't officially met them yet. People around here were either afraid of them or thought they were great, there didn't seem to be any in between.

How they hadn't been caught for the shit they were rumoured to get up to was beyond her, but she supposed, with them heading an organised crime group, they'd learned how to be clever. The police most probably monitored them, but if they couldn't get solid evidence to bring them in for questioning, it was no wonder they still gadded about like they did. Or, because there had always been leaders of estates in London, did the police just let them get on with it? Was there some kind of mutual agreement? Because wasn't it better that the leaders got rid of criminals to save the coppers the hassle?

Debbie came back. "Sorted. They'll be here soon."

"What are they like?" Lillibet sat on a stool in front of a breakfast bar.

"George and Greg? Oh, they're brilliant. Two of my best friends."

"Is it really true, what they do? All that killing and whatever? I mean, there have been so many people who've had their faces sliced—people reckon that's George. How do they get away with that?"

"I don't discuss what they get up to until I've been given the green light—that's for them to tell you if they want to. But you need to realise something. If they're going to help you, what you see and hear from now on, you've *got* to keep it to yourself. Yes, the police tend to turn a blind eye, probably so they don't have to admit the leaders are good at covering their arses, but it only takes a changing of the guard down the copshops, new superintendents or whatever, and everything could change. Someone's bound to want to play by the rules and take them down eventually, so what they do, how they do it—you can't tell anyone."

"I'm good at keeping secrets, don't worry."

Debbie looked at her funny and brought a coffee over, placing it on a coaster. "Want to elaborate on that?"

"If I did, it would mean I *can't* keep a secret."

Debbie smiled. "That's the correct answer. Unless the secret you keep will affect what the twins will be doing for you."

Lillibet shook her head. "No, it won't." Killing Stephanie had nothing to do with this. No one apart from her old colleagues at Fords' knew she'd been involved.

"Good." Debbie got on with making her own coffee.

"Sorry to have disturbed your evening."

Debbie laughed. "I wasn't doing anything much, just helping out in the pub. Moon's away in Amsterdam again, so I was filling time."

"Amsterdam? A holiday?"

"Business."

Lillibet got the sense she ought to mind her own. "I'll have to sort somewhere to stay until the killer's caught."

"You can either camp out here, or George and Greg will take you to one of their safe houses. Or better yet, you can come and stay with me at Moon's—I doubt the killer would think you'd go to another Estate. I'd say you won't be able to work, in case you're being watched, but that's not my call. The twins might feel you need to act as normal—maybe even use you as bait."

Lillibet's stomach dropped. "Bait? Bloody hell…"

"Don't worry, they'll assign someone to watch you all the time."

Lillibet rubbed her goosepimpled arms. "Did you see any cars in my street when you came to get me?"

"What, apart from the ones belonging to residents? Nobody sat inside any if that's what you're getting at."

"Which way did you come? He drove off towards the Plaza."

"Not that way. I came through the housing estate."

"Right."

The idea of that man parking at the Plaza and scoping out the people there… What if someone else waited for a taxi and he grabbed them? What if he was so angry Lillibet hadn't got into his car that he chose a random woman to take it out on?

Hello, Lillibet. You're next…

She prayed that was true, that he stuck to whatever list he'd made and no one else got killed. And she prayed the twins would find him sooner rather than later. Living on her nerves—she didn't think she could cope with that. It had been bad enough after Stephanie's death. Being questioned by the police again—or Cardigan's equivalent, The Brothers—was a daunting thought.

Chapter Two

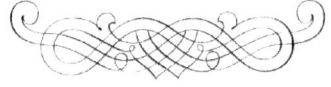

He couldn't contain his anger. It wasn't supposed to go like this. Lillibet was meant to get in his car and be killed, but it had gone wrong. Why had she shaken her head at him as she'd stood at the kerb? No, she hadn't been working, but the others, they'd gone with him anyway. Weren't they *all* money-hungry slags? Didn't they *all* want extra cash to fund their drug habits or other addictions? Feed their kids and put the leccy on? Filthy, the lot of them. Just like *her*.

Parked down a dark side street, he seethed, flexing his glove-covered hands. The leather creaked, reminding him how it had sounded when he'd gripped the cows' throats and choked them while staring into their wide eyes. Fear-filled eyes. Eyes that had red veins in them, growing wider because he'd squeezed so hard. He was a cliché, killing them because he couldn't kill *her*, but he didn't give a shit what label hung around his neck. It was better than the anvil that had dangled there when *she'd* been alive.

He leaned his head back and closed his eyes. Breathed in through the nose and out through the mouth. Calm, he must be calm. He couldn't approach the next one on the list if he was in this shit state. They'd sense he was off. That they needed to run.

His family knew he wasn't right. He'd tried to be 'normal' but didn't know what that was anymore. He managed to behave for short spates of time when everyone made it clear they were getting tired of his behaviour, but his messed-up mind always took over and he acted out again.

Pissing them off. Being irritating. Nasty. He shouldn't be like this now he was an adult, he should know better, yet here he was, prepared to kill again. To bring shame down on everyone who'd tried to do what was best for him.

His thoughts had only served to rile him up even more. He got out and switched number plates—in his rearview mirror, he'd clocked Lillibet staring at the other one, possibly memorising it. All of the plates he'd used belonged to regular punters in the various locations where the slappers worked—he'd written them down on the nights he'd sat in his car and watched. If anyone had remembered them and told the police, those men would be questioned. Maybe even get the blame for what he'd done.

Tomorrow night, he'd use a different car, one of many he could pick from. He'd planned this so well and for so long, nothing could go wrong. Even if CCTV picked up the motors, it didn't matter. He never ended his journey home where a camera could see where he'd finally gone. And all of the vehicles he chose had tinted windows.

Back in the car, his face itching from the woolly balaclava, he drove to Kitchen Street, breaking his own rule of selecting a woman while they were at work. But his little scout around at the Plaza after he'd been to Lillibet's house hadn't thrown up any prospective victims, and he needed to get this…this *thing* out of him, the urge to kill.

He cruised down the road, slowing by Sharny. She was number five on his list, the one who was supposed to die after Lillibet, the only two he'd selected from Kitchen. The first three, they'd worked in various other areas in the East End, and numbers six and seven were based on Debbie's Corner. Maybe he'd have to rethink that if Lillibet went running to The Brothers after what he'd done tonight. They'd be more vigilant.

I should never have left the note. I didn't do that with the others.

Still, while he had the time to snatch Sharny, he would, then never come back here again.

She approached the car, smiling, likely having checked the number plate in those stupid phones they all carried—or perhaps she'd seen the plate so many times down here before that she knew it off by heart. Why wasn't she querying that the plate didn't match the car, though? Huh, they must *all* be thick. There was so much emphasis on them knowing the plates that she'd failed to pick up the most obvious thing. Yes, the car was black, like the punter's, but it was the wrong shape.

He hoped she didn't notice that at the last minute and refuse to get in.

She rounded the bonnet and slid into the passenger seat, glancing away from him, tugging at the seat belt, not seeing he had a balaclava on. Trusting him, thinking he was the other man, the one who owned that plate.

He smirked, pressed a button, and drove off.

The click of the seat belt meeting the anchor filled his stomach with butterflies of excitement. She'd see him in a minute. She'd realise her mistake. He studied her out of the corner of his eye, and she was too busy digging in her handbag, producing a condom, to have spotted he wasn't the grey-haired old man who should have been driving this car.

He increased his speed.

"Bloody hell, Frank, slow down, will you?"

She stared at him then, her face showing her shock and confusion. She opened her mouth to either scream or say something, so he elbowed her in the face before she had a chance to shout at him to let her out. The crunch of her nose breaking satisfied him—she was like Mr Spencer now with a broken nose. He elbowed her again for good measure, going for her eye, so a tear would fall, and *that* would be like Mr Spencer, too. Mr Spencer brought comfort, and maybe, if Sharny looked like him, she'd bring comfort, too. It hadn't worked with the others, but there was always hope.

She cried out, hands to her face, and he nipped down a side street, parking next to a long brick wall at the rear of people's back gardens, gates spaced out. A few wheelie bins and black bags of rubbish marred the view, but that was to his advantage. Sharny would be posed beside a bin, ready for someone to find in the morning.

He took Mr Spencer out of his pocket and stood him on the dash. "You stay there and watch."

Sharny stared at the toy soldier and got hold of her senses. Went for the door handle. He shot his hand out and gripped her right wrist, keeping her in place. Engine off, he sighed. Why did they have to be so *difficult*?

"Sit still and behave," he said quietly.

With heaving breaths, she still snatched at the handle.

"It won't open. I've adapted it. Once it's closed, it locks until I press a little button to release it." He smiled at his bullshit. "Now then, if you do as you're told, I'll be happy."

He never said it would be all right or he wouldn't kill them, because that would be *outright* lying, not just a fib, and he'd had enough of that. Still, the phrase gave them the impression they'd be safer if they obeyed. That they might live.

Sharny was no different. She stared ahead, her free hand on her thigh, nails digging into her bare leg. She'd likely be pretending to obey him, but he wasn't stupid enough to believe she'd comply. Perhaps she thought he was a common or garden rapist or a punter who didn't want to pay. He reckoned they'd have been taught about those, what to do, and if they hadn't, they'd have experienced that type anyway.

"Where's Frank?" she whispered, her voice wobbly.

What an inane thing to say, considering the thousand other questions she could have asked. Why was Frank the first thing on her mind? Was he a nice man? Was she worried he'd been hurt? Did she think his car had been stolen?

Except it isn't his fucking car, you dumb bitch.

He took a deep breath to get rid of his annoyance. "I have no idea."

"So why are you in his car?"

"I'm not. You should have been more vigilant before you got in."

"Oh fuck, oh God…"

"Open the glove box."

She kept her hand where it was.

"I *said*, open the glove box. If you don't, it won't only be your nose and eye that are hurting."

She reached forward, fumbled, and the glove box opened.

"There's a good girl. Take out that cloth."

As it was dark, she probably couldn't see it, but she felt around all the same, taking out a microfibre; he'd chosen a bright-orange one this time.

"Put it in your mouth," he said.

She whimpered, dropped the cloth in her lap, and swung her arm round. He'd been expecting it so raised his to block the blow. He leaned close, taking hold of her nose and twisting the end. The pain must have been immense, as she screamed, choked on the agony and, because he was satisfied she understood he wasn't fucking about here, he let it go.

"It's better to be a good girl," he said, his voice low. "Bad girls get into situations like these. *She* did. If she'd have just done as that man had told her, she wouldn't have been cut so much. But she struggled, made a big fuss, and in the end, she died in misery. Distress. So much distress. Do you want to die like that?"

She shook her head.

"No, I didn't think you would. So put the cloth in your mouth."

She snatched it up and stuffed it in, anger pouring off her. At herself for not checking who he was when she'd got in the car? For realising she'd made such a big mistake? For putting her life at risk, night after night, when she should have been at home being good, looking after her kids?

If *she* had done that, he wouldn't be who he was now. Tortured, confused, with so much rage inside him that it drove him mad half the time. Before that man had knocked on the door, he'd been none the wiser about what *she* did. Then the truth had unfolded, and he'd been shown exactly what she'd been doing. He'd tried believing her, that she'd done it all for him, but that was a lie. She could have done a different job. She shouldn't have left him alone every night, scared out of his mind.

"Pull the lever down the side of your seat and lie back." He pinched Sharny's wrist to remind her he still held it, that despite her door being locked, she was going nowhere.

She leaned forward, poked about down the side, and the mechanism clunked. She rested back, daring to look at him. Not that she'd see much in the dark. Maybe the lighter skin around his eyes and mouth. The balaclava hid the rest. He couldn't see her clearly either. He usually put the interior light on when he got to this stage, but he was in a residential area and couldn't risk being seen. He may have tinted windows, but people would still be able to see him if they nosed out of their cosy houses.

He climbed on top of her, anticipating exactly what she did—she fought, her free hand coming up to slap at his head, and he laughed, the layer of balaclava weakening the sting of her strikes. He pushed down the wrist he held, knelt on it, and did the same with the other once he'd wrestled it under control. She created merry hell with the noise coming out of her, but the cloth dulled it.

He took his phone out and selected the recording he'd made. Pressed PLAY. Put the phone beside Mr Spencer. The tinkling wind chimes took him right back to childhood. To that night.

Hands around her throat, the leather gloves creaking, he squeezed.

She snorted, trying to breathe, bucking to tip him off her. He lessened his hold on her throat, waiting for her to suck in a huge lungful of oxygen through her nostrils. That sound always reminded him of the past, the rasp of it, how it grated on the air.

He squeezed again. Let go. *Rasp*. Squeezed. Let go. *Rasp*.

She grew limper, giving up the fight. It always happened this way, where they knew when they were beaten, when it was pointless to carry on fighting.

"Such a good girl at last, Sharny."

She seemed to come alive at that — he knew her name, and the implications of it must be streaking around in her head: *How does he know me? Has he been watching me? Does he know where I live?*

"I know a lot about you," he told her. "You've been living your life, completely unaware that I've been there, following, taking notes. You have children, don't you. Such a shame they're going to find out exactly who you are—and believe me, that's not going to be pleasant. I should know, I've been through it. But I can't help myself. You have to go no matter what they'll feel. Why should I be the only one to have suffered? I want to share my pain. I want everyone to know what *she* did to me."

He took his hands from her neck and pulled a flick-knife from his jacket pocket. He wished he could see her properly, see the skin part as he drew the blade down her face. See her breasts when he sliced her top down the middle to expose them, and when he carved into her chest above them, the blood flowing, her fear growing. But tonight had gone wrong because of Lillibet, so he'd make the best of it.

He got to work, her muffled cries filtering through the cloth in her mouth. Soon, she'd be silent, but for now, he'd carve away and live up to his new name.

Slasher.

Chapter Three

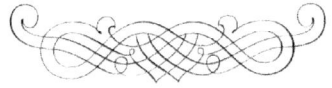

The wind chimes outside the front of the house tinkled in the wind. Billy Meyers hunched over on the sofa, hugging his knees, his chin propped between them. Mummy was out again, she went out every night, and he had to sit in the dark. Having lights on meant people might come and knock or ring the bell. It meant they'd know someone was in, and he wasn't supposed to be left on his own. Mummy said

she'd get into trouble if anyone found out. He'd be taken away from her.

The wind moaned again, a horrible monster, and his eyes stung. He cried a lot when Mummy wasn't there. He didn't like being alone, it scared him. Mummy said he should be used to it by now, but how could he get used to it when ghosts came out once it got dark? They roamed around the house, their footsteps loud, and the creaks where they opened doors trying to find him were the scariest. Mummy told him that was just the house settling, whatever that meant, but he didn't believe her. A settling house didn't tap on the walls. It didn't growl.

He looked at the DVD player. Seven o'clock. Time for dinner. The glowing blue numbers lit up the carpet beneath the TV cabinet. One of his toys lay there, Mr Spencer, a wooden soldier in royal-blue trousers and a red jacket with gold buttons. Mr Spencer had a funny hat on, too, the same as those men who guarded Buckingham Palace. A bearskin, Mummy called it. His face had chips in it where he'd been dropped so many times, the end of his nose snapped off. It looked like Mr Spencer was crying; one of the cheeks had a slither of pale-pink paint missing. While the soldier might be ugly to some because he wasn't perfect, Billy loved him.

He got off the sofa and picked him up, taking him to the kitchen. The oven, on low, had Billy's dinner inside it, and he had to wait to eat it—no taking it out before seven. He had a sandwich snack after school to tide him over. They didn't have a microwave, but he wished they did.

He stood Mr Spencer on the worktop. "You stay there and keep watch. If a ghost comes, shoot it with your gun."

Billy stuck his hands in the too-big heatproof gloves and opened the oven door. He reached in, gripped the plate with another upside-down on top, and put them on the hob. Door shut, he turned the dial to zero, immediately missing the light from inside the oven. Most days in winter, he sat in front of it and read his books until seven, but tonight the wind had scared him too much, the trees out the back swaying, their shadow branches dancing on the walls, the cupboards, clawed fingers. Mummy had forgotten to roll the blinds down, and he was too clumsy to pull the cord, he usually got it tangled, so he'd run into the living room to hide.

But it wasn't so dark after all—the moon was a big fat face tonight, and it shone through the window. He took the top plate off and carried his dinner to the table, putting it on the placemat Mummy had set out before she'd left. He shook the gloves off and sat, staring outside through the glass in the back door, checking if anyone watched. Sometimes, a man stood out the front beneath the streetlamp or sat in his car, and Mummy said they needed to watch out for him because he wasn't nice.

No man stood in the garden, so Billy ate his dinner. It was sausage and mash, peas on the side, the onion gravy a bit dried out at the edges. Mummy was good at cooking, and Billy never went without. Not food anyway. What he went without was having her home every night. He wished she was like other mummies who tucked him into bed and kissed his cheek after reading him and Mr Spencer a story, but she had to work to pay the bills and buy the food.

"I wonder what she does," he said to Mr Spencer.

The soldier didn't answer. Billy prayed he would. He wouldn't feel so lonely if Mr Spencer talked back.

He sipped some of the orange juice Mummy had left on the table—three little cartons with straws, two of them already gone. He had to drink them all before he went to bed else he'd piddle on the mattress while he was asleep if he didn't wee them all out in time.

He finished his dinner and took the plate and cutlery to the sink. Collected the other plate from the hob. Mummy had left bubbly water in the bowl, so he washed up his things and propped them on the drying rack. He put the placemat and oven gloves away, threw the cartons in the bin, and wiped the table with the bright-coloured dishcloth.

"All the rules followed," he said to Mr Spencer.

Now for a bath. He did exactly as Mummy had said—"Only use a little bit of water, Billy, or I'll worry you'll drown…" By the time he'd got out, dried himself, and put his pyjamas on, he was right on time. Quarter to eight.

Downstairs, he collected Mr Spencer from the kitchen and stopped at the sight of someone looking in through the window above the sink. It was the man who usually stood out the front. Billy gasped and squeezed the soldier tight, keeping still so he wasn't seen. But that moon, it was so bright…

The man tapped on the glass and brought his face closer to it, his nose squishing on the end. Billy held his breath, trying not to cry.

"Open the door." The voice, although muffled, was still clear enough.

Billy didn't move.

"What are you doing in there by yourself? Where's your mum?"

Billy couldn't stand it any longer. He ran into the living room, diving onto the sofa and clutching Mr Spencer in his aching hand. Tears burned and fell, coating his cheeks, and he closed his mouth to keep the noises inside. Mummy was going to be cross because the man had seen him. She'd be even more cross with herself for leaving the kitchen blinds open. She always muttered when she'd done something wrong, saying she was useless and should know better.

Another knock, louder, closer.

He must have gone round the front.

Billy hugged his knees. The wind chime tinkled, and the breeze whistled through the gaps in the old windows, the thick curtains growing a big belly in the middle, then settling straight again. He held Mr Spencer so hard his fingers hurt.

"You shouldn't be by yourself. I bloody **knew** *she was doing this!"*

Billy jumped. The voice had sounded so loud. He got up and crept to the living room door. Peered around the jamb. A cold waft of air came in—the letterbox flap was up, held there by fingers, two eyes beneath.

"She'll be in trouble with the police if they find out," the man said. "Look, I'm going to have to ring them. It's not right that she leaves you."

"No," Billy shouted. "They'll take me away!"

"Then I'll stay here until she comes home."

But it was winter. Wouldn't he catch a cold? Billy wished Mr Spencer was a real soldier so he could scare him away. Shoot him with the rifle he held against his chest.

"I've wanted to speak to you for such a long time. What's your name?"

This was a stranger, so Billy couldn't tell him. Strangers were bad.

"My mum never used to leave me alone," Stranger said. "She was there every night, and yours should be, too. What she does for a job, it's disgusting. She should be ashamed of herself."

"What does she do?" Billy hadn't meant to say that.

"She lets men put their willies inside her."

Billy frowned. Where did they put them? And wasn't that rude? Mummy said if anyone ever asked him to do rude things, he should tell a grown-up. Even if they only talked about it. Stranger must *be bad, then.*

"Go away," Billy said.

"I can't, not now I definitely know you're by yourself."

"My babysitter's just gone to the shop." He hoped Stranger believed him. It was what Mummy had told him to say if anyone ever spoke to him while she was out. She wouldn't get in so much trouble if he was only

on his own for a bit. He was eight anyway, a big boy, and she'd taught him to look after himself.

Billy stepped back, closed the lounge door, and walked over to the phone on the coffee table. Mummy had said he could ring her if it was an emergency, so he picked it up and pressed the number one—she'd programmed her number in there. She had a phone she carried with her all the time, and she had to put money on it for it to work.

"Billy?" she said, sounding scared, like she did if she thought he'd hurt himself.

"There's a man at the door," he muttered.

"Fuck. Sorry, I didn't mean to swear, that was naughty. Ignore him, okay? It's probably one of those people I told you about. You know, the ones just out of prison selling those cloths I buy."

"You didn't shut the blinds, and he was in the back garden, looking at me. Now he's talking through the letterbox, saying men put their willies in you."

"Shit. Shit! Did you speak to him?"

"I told him to go away. He said he knows you're not here."

"Oh God, what did you say?"

"The babysitter's up the shop."

"Good. Good boy. Give it a couple of minutes, and Kelsie will be there, all right? I'll phone her now."

Kelsie lived two doors down and stayed overnight if Mummy had to go away for work. She was sixteen and nice, and she let him watch telly way past bedtime.

"All right," he said.

Billy put the phone down, tiptoed over to the living room door, and opened it again. His stomach hurt—it always did if he was frightened. He peeked at the front door. The letterbox was shut, but Stranger's shape filled the patterned glass. Wide. Tall.

"He's still there," he said to Mr Spencer.

Billy waited…and waited. Where was Kelsie? The couple of minutes Mummy had said…it had gone past that, hadn't it?

Another shape came, getting bigger as it neared the door.

"Who are you?" Kelsie asked, her voice loud.

"The kid's dad. What the fuck are you doing, leaving him in there on his own?"

"I was gone ten minutes, God!"

Dad?

How come Stranger hadn't seen Kelsie leaving her house? Had she come out round the back and walked down the alley into the street?

"Tell Emma I'll be round tomorrow to talk to her about this," Stranger said.

"Why bother now when you haven't all his life?"

"Because I didn't know he existed until six months ago. Anyway, fuck off, I don't have to explain anything to you. It's none of your business."

"All right, keep your hair on."

"How come the house is always dark every time I come? Is he on his own every night?"

"Blackout curtains, but oh, it's none of your business. Piss off before I phone the police."

One of the shapes moved away, getting smaller, and a key scraped in the lock. The door opened, and Billy wanted a wee he was that worried it might be the stranger coming in. But Kelsie's hand stretched inside and felt for the switch—he recognised her ring—and the light came on. She walked in holding a Spar carrier bag, as if she'd really been to the shop, and shut the door.

"Okay, Billy?"

He nodded, even though he wanted to shake his head and tell her how scared he was. "Was that my dad?"

"So he says, but I doubt your mum would know anyway."

What did that mean?

"Come on, I'll read you a story in bed. Your mum said I have to stay until she gets back."

He climbed the stairs, happy to have the light on, to have Kelsie here. He wished she could be here every night, but Mummy said she couldn't afford it. In bed, the covers up to his chin, he scooted over so Kelsie could lie beside him. She took a book from the pile on his nightstand and opened it.

"Once upon a time…"

Billy closed his eyes, trying hard to listen to the story, but all he couldn't think about was Stranger. Billy had always wanted a dad, and if that man was his, why couldn't he see him? Christopher's dad saw him at weekends, and they went bowling and to McDonald's. Why couldn't Billy do that with his?

He didn't want to ask Mummy else she'd get upset, but he really wanted to know the answer to that. Maybe, if Stranger came back, he'd ask him.

Chapter Four

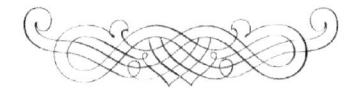

The tension in the kitchen seemed to squeeze George's throat. Anger built inside him, and if he were honest, the fact he hadn't been able to catch the Slasher yet scored a hole inside him. He felt useless, and it didn't sit well. Now Lillibet had told them her story, he felt even worse. Who the fuck *was* this bloke? What gave him the right to go around killing innocent women? And why was he doing it?

George glanced at Greg who leaned against the wall in Debbie's kitchen. "This wanker's got to be stopped before he hurts someone else."

"It's all very well saying that, bruv, but we've been looking for him since he started." Greg pinched his chin. "He's a sneaky little bastard. Janine's not having much luck either."

George had been getting regular updates from their copper, Janine, who'd passed on information about the investigation. The three victims so far, Lola Jennings, Verity Smith, and Olivia Lock, had all been Cardigan residents, so George and Greg had visited their next of kins to hand over money to help with the funeral arrangements when the bodies were finally released. Janine had said they were evidence and would be kept for some time yet.

All of the ladies had at least one kid, and they'd been working on the streets to earn extra money to get by. Their day jobs hadn't paid much, basically minimum wage efforts, and with bills skyrocketing, they'd been forced to make the decision to sell sex. None of them had known each other, nor had they worked on the same patches. It appeared their selection had been at random—unless it was a punter they'd all been with. Some men visited different patches, maybe so their cars weren't spotted in regular locations.

"I hate him being out there," George said, "planning to kill again." He looked at Lillibet. "How tall was he?"

"Short. Maybe five-six, something like that."

"What about his build?"

"Slim."

"So we could be talking a young lad here." George shook his head.

Teenagers had become so daring since he'd been one. In his day, the bold buggers were few and far between, like him and Greg. These days, every other kid had an attitude. This current generation baffled him, how they acted so entitled, getting upset if they didn't get their own way. Was the Slasher one of them? Had the dead women upset him, so he was teaching them a lesson?

Debbie leaned against the worktop and folded her arms. "Just because he might be young, or small, doesn't mean he's not capable of doing harm. This is worrying if he's basically a lad. He's got to be screwed up if he's committing this type of murder, say, in his twenties. Don't serial killers tend to be older?"

"But he *could* be older," Greg said. "He could have been thinking about doing this for years before he finally found the guts to do it."

Lillibet shivered. "How does he know my name? It makes me think he's a punter."

Debbie held a finger up. "Before I forget, have you looked into all the men on our database?"

George tutted. "Of *course* we have. What do you take us for? Them being cleared by Janine as safe doesn't mean they are."

"Which makes us having a database a bit pointless if one of them is the killer," Debbie said.

Greg flexed his fingers. "No, it doesn't. It gives us a long fucking list of people to look through if any of the girls get hurt. It narrows things down. We've spoken to every punter, Janine has an' all, and they've got solid alibis."

"So you gave Janine our list," Debbie said.

"Yep."

"How did she explain getting her hands on *that*?"

"She said one of the working girls kept notes and handed it over. She couldn't exactly put you in the shit by revealing to her boss that you run girls out there, could she."

"That's what I was worried about." Debbie collected their coffee cups and loaded them in the dishwasher.

George racked his brain, trying to think of a way to catch this bloke. "The easiest option is for Lillibet to be bait."

"No," she said, hugging herself.

"I knew you were going to say that, George." Debbie put a tablet in the dishwasher. "You'd better have a fucking good plan to watch her, because otherwise, I'm not having one of my girls put in danger."

"You'll be with her." George sat at the breakfast bar beside Lillibet and stared her in the eye. "All you need to do is stand on Kitchen like you usually do. I don't want you going with punters—if they ask for you, say no. But I want the names of all the ones who *do* ask for you. You'll go home at the end of the shift, as usual. Debbie will stay with you. I'll also get two of our bodyguards to kip at your place. If the Slasher breaks in, he'll get a rude surprise."

Lillibet thought about it. "Will they have guns?"

43

"Yep. If I ask Maxwell and his brother, Nate, they'll bring their attack dog, Scout. He's a rottweiler and can be nasty if he has to be. He'll bite the fucker's hand off." George could tell he hadn't persuaded her. "Think about it. If you'd got in his car earlier, you'd be dead by now. You wouldn't have had the foresight that someone's after you because no note would have been left. This way, you know damn well you're next, and the quickest way to find him is for you to keep doing things the same way. When's your next day off? That's important—all the others were killed on those days."

"Tomorrow because I work weekends."

"Good, that gives us a chance to get everything in place."

"But what if he's watching my house and he sees two men and a dog going in there? And Debbie? You can bet he already knows I live alone."

"Because he'll want to pick you up elsewhere, like he tried to do tonight, and everyone can go into your house round the back. You'll go to The Angel—if he's following you, he'll know where you are—and this time, we'll catch him."

"I don't like this," she said. "So many things could go wrong. I'd rather just go away somewhere until it's all over."

"Until he's caught for killing someone else, you mean." George was being a bastard, piling their guilt on her, but she didn't realise what a slick operation they ran and how quickly the bastard could be rounded up if she just played ball. No, he didn't usually like putting women in the firing line, but the murders had been brutal, and if Lillibet doing what he'd asked meant it saved more lives, why wasn't she prepared to do it?

"I'm frightened," she said. "Before I worked on Kitchen, I sat at a desk, for God's sake. I had no idea about dodgy punters or how some of them could get rough. I went into this thinking I could have sex, be dropped back on the street, and that would be the end of it. I was naïve, telling myself it'd be no different to sleeping around, which I'd done before. But it *is* different. Some of these men have agendas. Some of them get obsessed and only want me. And now there's the Slasher, who's chosen me out of hundreds. Why? What's so special about me?"

"I don't know," George said. "He doesn't even have a type. All the victims so far have had different colour hair. None of them have similar faces. It seems like he's got a beef with sex workers who have kids, that's all."

"That's all?" Lillibet shook her head. "You say it like it's nothing. And I don't have kids, so he's picked me for another reason."

"I didn't mean it to come across that way. What I'm saying is you're *not* special, okay? And that should make you feel better because you weren't chosen to match his ideal. He just picked you randomly."

"But he still picked her," Greg said. "Come on, you've got to admit this is scary shit for her. A bloke in a balaclava comes to your house and leaves a note saying you're next, then you go and tell the two people who are supposed to help you, and one of them insists you go back out there to lure him in? Give her a chance to digest it, for fuck's sake."

"Sorry, Lillibet," George said. "I didn't put myself in your shoes."

"No, you didn't." She rubbed the back of her neck. "I'm bricking it. Worrying that I won't be saved in time. I mean, if you want me to go to The

Angel and stand there as if I'm having a good time, where will you be? What if he snatches me and you don't get to me in time?"

"We will, trust me."

"There are so many things that could go wrong."

George sniffed. "Would it make you feel better if we brought Janine, our copper, in on it? If she's there, too?"

"Marginally."

"Have a think on it," George said. "Debbie will pack a bag and go home with you tonight. In the meantime, I'll check that number plate."

"Already done it just before you arrived," Debbie said. "It's Frank's."

"Frank who?"

"Solloway."

George chuckled. "Well, it won't be him. He's about twenty stone and nearly six foot so doesn't match the description. We'll go and speak to him anyway. Someone he knows might have borrowed his car." He sent messages to Maxwell and Nate, telling them to get their arses round Lillibet's but keep out of sight and watch the street before they approached the back door—and to wait for Debbie and Lillibet to turn up first before they went inside using their lock pick. "Right, everything's sorted. We'll get off and speak to Frank." He laid a hand on Lillibet's shoulder. "You're doing the right thing."

"I'd better be, but I want you to know I'm doing this with reservations."

He smiled and walked out of the flat, getting in the BMW. Greg must have stayed behind to reassure her, as he got in the passenger side a couple of minutes later.

"You're as subtle as a sledgehammer, bruv." Greg clipped his seat belt in. "The poor cow's crapping herself, and in you go, not thinking about anything but catching the killer."

"Yeah, well, my dander's up. She's been threatened, and I don't like it."

"Neither do I, but be a bit more mindful in future. Think before you speak. Like Debbie's just said, this is dangerous. We need to have an airtight plan before we let Lillibet go to The Angel."

"We'll get loads of our men on it. We'll all sit and wait for him." George accessed the database on their phone and found Frank's address. "We'll likely be getting him out of bed."

"Who cares?"

"True."

George reversed out of the car park and headed to Frank's. He was so single-minded sometimes that he forgot to take people's feelings into consideration. It was only now that he imagined Lillibet shitting herself about having to go home, to the place where the Slasher's note had landed on her mat. The house would feel like it had been violated, even though the killer hadn't been in there. She'd remember her fear on reading those words.

"God, I'm such a dick sometimes," he muttered.

"Finally sinking in what you've done, is it?"

"Yeah."

"Good."

George swerved around a corner and parked outside number sixteen, behind Frank's motor. The hairs on the back of his neck rose with him thinking about that car being used to try and pick Lillibet up. He threw himself out of the BMW and up the garden path, walloping the shit out of the front door with three hard bangs of his fist.

Greg came and stood beside him. "Could you be any louder?"

"Yep." George battered the door again.

A top window next door flew open, and a woman poked her head out. "What the fuck are you doing, making all that racket? It's past midnight."

"Where's Frank?" George asked.

"In the air by now, most likely."

"What?"

"He's been in the Canaries. His flight was due to take off at eleven."

George processed that. "So he's been away?"

"Yeah."

"Who are you?"

"His sister. I don't need to ask who *you* are."

Her derision rankled him; what a cheeky cow to be so rude to *them*, The Brothers. Should he bollock her for it? *Nah, leave it.* "Has anyone driven his car since he left?"

"Nope."

"So it hasn't moved from that spot?"

"Nope."

"How long has he been away?"

"Ten days. What's all this about?"

George ignored that. "When does he land?"

"About half three in the morning, our time."

"Right." George stomped off to the car and flung himself in the driver's seat. When Greg got in, he said, "Did you believe her, that the car hasn't moved?"

"I didn't pick up that she was lying."

"I'm going to ring Janine, see what she has to say about it." He prodded her icon on the phone screen and put it on speaker.

It rang three times, then she said, "This had better be good…"

"What do you know about any cars the first three Slasher victims got into?"

"All number plates in those vicinities have been logged and checked. Something interesting cropped up, though. Three flagged vehicle plates belonged to cars that didn't match the make — one for a Kia, one a Volkswagen, and the other a Honda. Yet the cars on camera were different. Each car owner, when questioned, had admitted they used sex workers but had been elsewhere on those nights. Their alibis checked out — and their actual number plates had been recorded exactly where the men said they'd been. The killer's using punters' plates, so he's definitely watching the women."

"Clever bastard." George clenched his fist. "What cars were caught on camera, the ones used to abduct the girls?"

"An Audi, a Tesla, and a Bentley, so vastly different."

"Someone who owns more than one car—someone with a lot of money."

"Yes. That's being checked at the moment. We're trying to find one name associated with those three vehicles."

"What if he doesn't own them all and he's borrowed them?"

"Then whoever gets their cars back will notice blood on the seats—do you think those people aren't going to phone that information in? Fibres from the seats of an Audi, Tesla, and Bentley were found on the clothes of each victim. I'm betting the Slasher owns all the cars."

"Hmm. Okay."

"Was there a reason you asked about it?"

"Yeah." He explained about Lillibet and how they were sitting outside Frank Solloway's. "But he's currently flying home from holiday. Been gone ten days, so it's another number plate clone."

"Shit. So the Slasher's on the prowl again. What do you plan to do now?"

"Set him up. We need to fine-tune the logistics, but we'll let you know when you'll be needed."

"That's going to be a tricky one for me to explain as to why I was in The Angel, with you two and God knows how many of your men."

"Nah, you just happened to be out with Cameron and saw shit going down."

"For that to be plausible, we're going to have to eat there, so I'll need plenty of time before you set up the sting so we just happen to be leaving when it all goes down, then I have to step in."

"Fine. Laters." George popped the phone in the cup holder.

"Where are we off to now?" Greg asked.

"Home. We've got plans to make."

Chapter Five

The next morning, Janine stood in a wide alley wedged between the high walls of people's back gardens. A three sided tent had been erected over the body and the wheelie bin—the victim rested against the wall, sitting up, so the rear of the tent couldn't be put in place without disturbing the crime scene. A flap of material covered the gap between the roof and the top of the brick wall, to give complete privacy.

DS Colin Broadly stood beside her, both of them in protective outfits. Jim, the pathologist, waited patiently for the last few photos to be taken. Some had been snapped before the tent had gone up to get a wider view of the scene, but today's photographer, Rufus, concentrated on close-ups now the eyes of the prying public were out of sight.

Many residents had come out when Mary Tomkins had screamed at seven-thirty a.m. She'd paused in putting her rubbish in the wheelie bin, seeing the body in all its naked, sliced-up glory. A few people loitered outside the tent still, as did Mary, who'd refused to return to her house, convinced the killer had nipped in there while her back was turned—PCs had gone in to check, but there was no telling some people. Residents hung around beyond the cordons, a couple of phones up and ready to record the goings-on. Janine had asked them to go home, to not put anything on social media out of respect for the victim's family—the next of kin hadn't been notified yet, and for them to find out via SM that their loved one had been murdered wasn't something she wanted to happen.

She sighed. A crime scene wasn't just dealing with the body, it was other logistics as well, and it irritated her. Like everything seemed to lately.

Concentrate on this, not the bloody public.

The deceased's clothes lay in a haphazard pile on the ground, and a blue handbag had yet to be inspected for ID. The shoes were likely beneath the pile, the same as where the other victims' stilettos had been. Lola, Verity, and Olivia hadn't deserved to die. Outside of their profession they'd been mums just trying to make a living.

Rufus stood back, indicating he'd finished for the time being, and Jim got on with his initial checks, noting things down on the paper chart on his clipboard. He was old-school and didn't bother with an electronic way of recording things until he'd got back to his office.

"It's got to be the Slasher," Colin said. "All of the others had the same words on their chests. The same markings."

"*These* words are a bit wonky, though." Janine stared at them. "Reckon he did them in the dark?"

Colin shrugged. "However he did it, he's a nutter."

The dead woman's cheeks had an X cut into one, a Y on the other. The previous three victims had the same, and Janine's team had gone down the obvious route of it pointing to chromosomes. That search hadn't thrown up anything but confusion, questions, and Janine had to wonder if the X and Y meant something else.

She moved her attention to the chest. LYING BITCH had been written, and below that, seemingly random stabs to the breasts. The areolas had been sliced in a plus sign, the centre point of the + the nipples. These slices were deep, exposing flesh and fat globules. Blood, now dried, had dribbled sideways, so the victim had been reclining when the killer had gone to town on her.

The stomach had a crude serpent carved on it—the team had already established what that might mean. Apparently, serpents represented lies, temptation, and deception. Something to do with the part the creature had played in Eden when it had convinced Eve to eat the fruit of the Tree of Knowledge. Did the killer feel the victims had lied to him, deceived him in some way? Had he met with them, thinking there might be a potential relationship in the offing, only for him to discover they were sex workers? Or was he punishing them for tempting him so he didn't have to face the fact he'd *chosen* to proposition them? Or did this follow the pattern she'd seen many times when women were killed one after the other in what was called a spree—they hadn't done *anything* to him, but they symbolized someone who had? If so, why the different hair colour? There had to be another reason they'd been selected.

It was clear that because he hadn't been able to get to Lillibet, he'd picked someone else. Lillibet, the poor cow, when she found out about this, would probably blame herself.

Janine would like to say the rest of the body was untouched by a blade, but the labia and vulva had been ruined. They no longer resembled what they were, too many stabs and slash marks, leaving a pulpy, fleshy, bloody mess. If this lady's postmortem showed what the others had, her vaginal opening would also have been attacked with that knife, the same inside her.

So someone was angry these women had chosen a certain profession? The hatred in those slices, all the marks and cuts, the wording, the serpent, pointed to that.

CCTV had been trawled near the spots where the previous victims had worked, but of course, they hadn't stood anywhere they could be caught on camera for soliciting. While taking money for sex wasn't illegal in the UK, touting for business in public, including from people in cars, was, so these ladies would have been careful where they'd conducted business.

The investigation had led the team to where the victims' patches had been, though. With the promise that no one would be in trouble for talking to the police, the information had been given freely by the working girls regarding Lola, Verity, and Olivia. All of them had been murdered on their night off. Now she'd had time to think about it, Janine didn't buy that he hadn't known they were sex workers, that his selection had been random and it was a coincidence they'd all had the same profession. He'd been watching them, following them.

Sheila Sutton, the scene manager, came into the tent. "Just been informed by a PC doing house-to-house enquiries that someone parked out here last night around eleven. They said it was a dark vehicle and saw it when they closed their bedroom curtains."

"Didn't they think that was odd?" Janine asked.

"No. Apparently, a bloke parks there a lot—there's a drug issue around here, one of the sellers deals from his car. The resident assumed it was him. She'd been out before to tell him not to peddle there, but he threatened her, so she's been keeping her nose out."

"Did she note how long they were there for?"

"No. She got into bed and fell asleep quickly. One other person saw the car—again, they were going to bed—and they heard an engine start about half eleven, so I assume the whole carving and murder took half an hour." Sheila stared at the body. "Strangulation marks. A single stab to the carotid. Same as the others."

"Hmm." Jim finished his perusal. "Awful way to go, especially as I believe those wounds were created while they were alive."

"Do you think the cloths in the mouth have significance?" Sheila asked Janine. "This one's bright orange, and the others were yellow, green, and blue respectively."

"Maybe, or he could have bought a multicoloured pack and is using them one by one. It might be something as mundane as that."

Jim gestured at Sheila. "Can you have a look in the handbag for me?"

Sheila changed her gloves, picked the bag up, and peered inside. "Large evidence bag a sec, please."

Jim provided one, opening it.

Sheila placed the handbag inside then brought a purse out. She flipped it open. "Credit card in the plastic window slot. Miss S Baker." She checked behind it, taking another card out. A driver's license, the picture resembling the dead woman. "Sharny Baker."

"Okay, I'll get on that." Colin left the tent.

"And I'll go and have a quick word with Mary." Janine walked out, changed from her protectives by the cordon, and put fresh booties on. She dipped beneath the police tape and approached a blonde woman standing with a PC. "Mary Tomkins?"

"Yes."

"I'm DI Janine Sheldon. Sorry for putting you through this again, but I need to ask some questions…"

They discussed what had happened and at what time. If the car had driven off at half eleven, that meant Sharny had been out in the elements for eight hours when Mary had found her. Rigor would have set in while everyone slept. The natural process stopped for no one, least of all the poor murdered woman.

"Thank you for your time." Janine went back to the cordon and strode to Colin now he'd finished on the phone. "Any luck?"

He stripped his protective suit and mask off. "The NOK's her mother, Alice Baker. Slightly creepy, this, but she lives in the street that backs onto the body."

"Oh shit, so she could have spoken to PCs already and have no idea it's her daughter who's dead. That's rotten. Come on, we'll go round there now."

Janine led the way towards the top of the T the alley formed with the road, where there was a row of shops and a playing field. Several police vehicles had parked there, and another crowd had gathered. Janine ignored the stares and marched round to the mother's street.

"What's the number?" she asked Colin.

He trotted to catch up. "Seven."

"Not far to go, then."

Janine glanced at the house. A woman in her fifties, swaddled in a red padded coat, stood talking to her neighbour over the dividing garden fence. Two boys kicked a football between them on the grass. Shit, were they Sharny's sons?

Janine approached the gate and held up her ID, giving their names. "Alice Baker?"

Red Coat nodded. "I've just given my statement to one of the plods. I've got nothing else to say because I didn't see anything. Beck did, though."

"Beck?"

"Me," the neighbour said. "I saw a dark car when I went to bed."

Janine smiled. "Ah yes, I've been told about that." She turned to Alice. "Can we come in for a chat?"

"What for? My daughter will be here in a minute to pick the kids up."

Janine often dealt with awkward people, George Wilkes being top of the list, but she wasn't in the mood today and really needed to break the news so she could crack on. "Is it possible for you to watch the lads for a few minutes, Beck?"

The woman nodded.

Alice rolled her eyes. "Fuck's sake. I didn't *see* anything. Just because it was right outside my back gate, doesn't mean I'm out there being nosy at all hours." She turned and pushed her front door open. "Stay with Beck, kids. I won't be long. And no fucking her about, got it?"

In the living room, Janine prepared herself. Colin took the opportunity to have a seat—rude when an offer hadn't been made, but that was him all over—and Alice stood by the window, keeping an eye on the boys. Janine pondered whether the Slasher had left Sharny at her mother's on purpose. If he had, then he'd tailed her at some point to know Alice lived here. Had he seen Sharny dropping the boys off before work?

"What's this all in aid of?" Alice asked. "Is it because she was left against my wall? It's not my fault, is it. I heard Mary from the other side of mine found her."

Why hadn't Mary recognised Sharny if she lived next door to her mother? Yes, the face had been slashed, but people would still know who she was.

"Does she know your family well?" Janine asked.

"Not really, she's only been here about two months. She's barely in. Works all hours. A nurse."

"I see."

"Why do you need to know?"

"Would you mind sitting down for me, Alice?"

The woman finally pulled her gaze from the children. "Look, just say what you've got to say then go."

Fair enough. "Based on the ID inside a purse found in the deceased's handbag, we have reason to believe the woman is your daughter, Sharny."

Alice barked out a laugh. "You're kidding, right? Sharny isn't a prosser, and the Slasher's only after them, isn't he?"

"We have yet to look into Sharny's life, but yes, he targets sex workers. What did Sharny tell you she does?"

"Overnight shifts at Sainsbury's, a shelf stacker."

"Which Sainsbury's?"

"The one on the roundabout just before the turning onto this estate."

"Right." *I'll get PCs to go there.* "While I appreciate you may think it isn't your daughter, we'll need a formal identification—unless you'd prefer us to go down the DNA route, which is highly understandable, given the facial injuries you may not want to see."

Alice appeared to enjoy the prospect of viewing a dead person, as though it gave her life a bit of excitement. "I'll go and have a gander at her now if you like, saves all the hassle of me going down the morgue or whatever. Then you'll see it isn't her. Honestly, she'll be here in a minute. She'd better be anyway. I need those kiddies picked up. I'm going out for lunch with Beck later."

"We'll go via the back garden," Janine said—she'd smooth it over with the DCI later about letting Alice enter the tent. "Less people to see you, then."

"What do I care if they see me?"

Would she enjoy being seen? Blimey. "I need to go first, because I have to get you some outerwear before you leave your garden. The same for us."

"Whatever."

Janine led the way and, at the gate, she requested protectives. Suitably togged up, including a forensic suit each, they moved to the tent entrance. Janine linked her arm with Alice's and guided her in. Colin remained outside.

Alice stared at the body.

Her scream was all the answer Janine needed.

Chapter Six

With Lillibet seemingly stuck to her side, Debbie stood on Kitchen Street, a crowd of women in front of her. Everyone's breaths clouded in the air, and coats covered top halves, although plenty of bare leg showed, despite the chilly weather. Those from the night shift had returned at her request so she could speak to them all at once. She'd been telling them extra watchers were being brought in, personal alarms would be distributed if they didn't already have them, and advising on how to stay safe when they weren't at work. Lillibet had explained what had happened to her the previous night, and many of the girls were shaken. Who could blame them? Debbie was, too. The perils of life working the streets had never left her, and she doubted they ever would.

She frowned, drawn away from the discussion. Janine pulled up and got out of her car with Colin. The twins must have got hold of her and passed on what Debbie and Lillibet had planned for this morning—Debbie had put on a short skirt so it appeared as if she was available for sex; she had to look the part. She'd shadow Lillibet all day. This little act was to make the killer think he hadn't spooked her.

"Two secs." Debbie walked over to the officers.

Cameron, Janine's bodyguard boyfriend, had also parked up but stayed in his vehicle. Debbie had found out that he was still guarding the copper until all members of the perverted group, The Network, had been rounded up. Janine had a target on her back, despite the man who ran the organisation being out of the picture.

"Err, what's going on?" Debbie asked.

"We're not here to shut things down. We'll turn a blind eye that soliciting is going on. We've got to speak to the women," Janine said quietly. "One of them has copped it."

"*What?*" Debbie's heart sank. Had the Slasher moved on to someone else like Lillibet had predicted? *Shit*. "Who?"

"Sharny Baker."

Debbie closed her eyes for a moment. Sharny was her night-time street manager, and Debbie had grown to like her a lot. Things wouldn't be the same without her. One of the others had not long said Sharny hadn't come back after she'd gone off with a punter about ten to eleven last night, but they'd assumed she'd asked him to take her home once she'd been with him as she'd mentioned not feeling too bright. She'd had a bad tummy and a headache.

From now on, Debbie would insist that all women clocked off via a WhatsApp chat so everyone else could see who was at work and who wasn't—and whether to be worried. She kicked herself for not doing that before, but the last thing she'd expected was to have some bloke running round killing working girls.

"Shit. Was it the Slasher?" she asked to confirm her fears.

"Afraid so."

As Debbie was unsure whether the twins had told Janine anything, she thought it best to tell her about Lillibet anyway. At least then Janine could act shocked in front of Colin. "There's something you need to know."

"What..." Janine slanted her eyes at her DS, a warning for Debbie to be careful what she said in front of him.

I'm not stupid! "Lillibet, the blonde over there in the black leather jacket, she saw who she thinks was the Slasher last night." Debbie explained everything, although from Janine's expression, she already knew. Maybe Debbie repeating the information while Colin stood there was just what Janine needed. "She rang me, and I picked her up." It was awkward not being able to speak freely about The Brothers, but Colin didn't appear to be buggering off anytime soon.

Janine seemed to pick up on Debbie's annoyance. "Colin, can you make a start with the questions, please?"

He tutted and ambled off.

Janine whispered, "Ignore him, he hates work."

"I gather the twins filled you in."

Janine patted her trouser pocket. "Shit, I didn't switch my burner on this morning to see if they've told me anything else. I got the call from the station about Sharny just as I was leaving my house to pick Colin up, so I forgot. Give me a minute while I see if they've sent me any messages with updates." She got back in her car.

Debbie wandered over to the two watchers who stood over the road. The one who'd done the night shift flushed, as if he waited for her to give him a bollocking.

"Thanks for waiting for me to get to you. What did you see last night, if anything?" she asked him.

Keenan shrugged. "Nothing untoward. All number plates were in the database. All plates matched the colours of cars."

"What about the makes?"

"It was dark…"

She'd let him off on that one. "When Sharny got into her last vehicle, how did she seem?"

"Fine because it was Frank's."

"Which Frank?"

"Solloway."

Debbie already knew that but wanted to double-check. He was a nice bloke. Often drank in The Angel. "Right, so nothing to worry about there. Hang on. Did anything stand out as off last night?"

Keenan sighed. "If there was, I'd have phoned it in. That's what I'm paid for."

Debbie gave him a tight smile. He'd got her back up. She didn't let anyone speak to her like that these days, so she geared herself up to tear him a new one. "I know you're tired, having to come back out when you'd only just got in bed, but being rude to me isn't on. For your information, Sharny is *dead*, and I don't appreciate your tone. I'm the one who pays your wages, so you'd be better off remembering that if you want to keep your job."

His eyes widened. "Sharny? Fuck! *I* didn't know, did I?"

"No, but it still doesn't mean you can speak to me like shit because you're knackered. You knew what you'd signed up for when you took this post. If I need you, you come, simple as that, you don't whinge about it."

The daytime watcher shook his head. "Poor Sharny."

Debbie huffed out a breath. "I know. The twins' copper will be asking you questions soon, so don't mention The Brothers if that bloke over there is with her. He doesn't know she's their plod, okay?"

The men nodded.

"If you think of anything, get hold of me, George, or Greg." Debbie stalked off to Janine's car and waited, her cheeks hot from her flare of anger.

Janine got out. "Okay, I'm up to date with everything. Nothing new reported. Sorry that us being here is going to stop the women earning money, but we really need to get cracking."

Debbie nodded and walked with her towards the group. "I'll take Lillibet to The Angel for a bit, you can talk to her there."

"Okay, see you later. I'll try and lose Colin."

"Easily done if I offer him a free cooked breakfast. He can eat that at a table while we chat at the bar."

They laughed despite the circumstances, and Janine got on with asking questions.

Debbie jerked her head at Lillibet. They sat in her car, and Debbie drove off.

"Did Colin say anything to you all as a group?" Debbie asked.

"No, he took Gabby off to one side. Why?"

Debbie pulled over, parking outside a row of council terraces. She had news to deliver and didn't want to be driving while she did it. Lillibet might need a cuddle.

"It's Sharny. The Slasher got to her last night."

"*What*? Oh God, I *knew* it. Didn't I *say*?"

Debbie nodded. "I'm sorry, love, but it isn't your fault, so don't go blaming yourself."

"Poor cow." Lillibet thumped her thighs. "This bloke's got to be stopped. I didn't want to be bait, but I'll bloody do it now without complaining. Take me back to Kitchen Street."

"We'll go later. Janine's going to come and speak to you at The Angel. If he's watching, it'll look like we've been told to leave by her, so don't worry."

"Where would he be watching from, though? We've been out there since seven and haven't seen anyone other than people going to work or regular punters."

"Think about how Crook kept an eye on you all."

Lillibet let out a long breath. "From his flat with that bloody telescope."

"Exactly. We can't assume the Slasher isn't doing something like that."

Debbie drove away again, glad Moon wasn't around to know she'd agreed to put herself in danger. Yes, she was still her own woman, she wouldn't let him coddle her to the degree she didn't have a say in her own life, but her fella was overprotective and would go off on one if she was harmed during all this. Maybe she should tell him so he could send someone to watch over them. She shook her head. No, he'd pick Alien or Brickhouse, and they weren't exactly inconspicuous men. Too big, tall, and wide.

Just as she turned into the street where The Angel stood, she caught sight of a car following in her rearview mirror. The twins had already thought of protecting them, she should have known they would. Ichabod, the manager at Jackpot Palace, raised a hand to his forehead in a salute. He did surveillance for the twins from time to time and was rumoured to be the best at it.

She parked down the side of the pub and ushered Lillibet into the bar. They sat at the end farthest from the door so she could keep an eye out. The Angel opened at half eight these days, people coming in for a full English, so the crowd was different to later in the day. She clapped eyes on Sonny Bates who usually worked for the twins at The Eagle, picking up information there, but here he was, likely sent to look out for anyone grabbing food in between creepily observing the women on the corner. For all she knew, the Slasher could have been in here several times while picking out his victims.

Debbie smiled as Ichabod came in and sat at a small table beside the door. She whispered to Lillibet to let her know two men had their backs, that The Brothers were looking after them, and the woman visibly relaxed.

"What if the Slasher sees we've got a tail all the time, though?" Lillibet asked.

"Ichabod is too discreet to get noticed, and Sonny will stay in here, listening. Want a coffee?"

Lillibet nodded, glancing round, fear in her eyes, likely wondering whether the man they wanted to catch was in here right now.

Debbie shivered. She'd just thought the same thing.

Chapter Seven

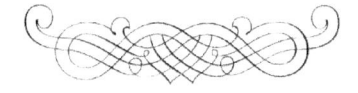

Slasher had slept like a baby. He always did after he'd got rid of a woman. It gave him a sense of peace, taking slags out of the equation, and he wished he'd done this a long time ago instead of suffering in brooding silence or acting the prick with his family. All those years of torment when he could have been feeling like this. Super-charged and on cloud nine. Happy.

The problem was, the time between his highs wearing off and the need to do it again had shortened. Google had told him it would do that, but he hadn't expected it to happen so soon. His urges had taken hold faster last time, which was why he'd gone for Lillibet a week after Olivia. How quickly would he want to kill Lillibet now? Tomorrow? The day after? When her body was found, would the police wonder why he'd chosen her when she didn't have any kids?

He straightened his tie and studied himself in the mirror. No one would think it was him who'd done this. Too short, too wiry, some little weed who people barely glanced at. They'd imagine the Slasher to be some big beefy bloke, well able to overpower women. What some didn't quite get was a balaclava put the fear of God into his victims, and all thoughts of his size went out of the window when they were presented with imminent death, his knife blade getting closer and closer to their breasts.

He was supposed to pop his head into work today, show his face at a meeting, but he wouldn't bother. It wasn't like he had to answer to anyone, was it, and he wasn't really needed when it came to making decisions. His father had taken early retirement and handed the business down to Slasher's younger half-brother, Darren, who dealt with things day to day. Slasher was there to cosign deals and attend board meetings, but other than that, he'd never had to do much. Darren was the star of the show, Slasher there in name only.

Another thing that pissed him off.

Money landed in his bank account for doing very little, and he was free to pursue whatever he wanted, which was running a little setup from his triple garage round the back of his home where he tinkered with cars—he'd been to college and whatnot to learn how to be a mechanic, and it was a hobby more than his job, so he had the freedom to do…this. His regular garage, tacked onto the side of the house, was where he kept his Merc. He also valeted and offered a number plate service, all pretty handy, considering. Although he used gloves when working, couldn't abide grease under his fingernails.

The vehicles he'd used when killing the women were those in for repairs, and he had some industrial-strength cleaning fluid to clean the interiors afterwards. While the blood would still be there if forensics tested it beneath those weird lights of theirs, visibly, it was gone. What person would suspect their mechanic had murdered women in their vehicles if splashes of blood weren't on their seats? Nobody.

Dad had bought him a house, the Merc, and paid the bills, trying to make up for the eight years he hadn't been in Slasher's life, or maybe it was to try and get him to behave like a normal person. A bribe. The man showered him with gifts and money.

I'm not complaining.

He left the house in an Audi, a false plate on. He drove to Kitchen Street, alarmed two people in suits stood there, a man and a woman, speaking to the girls. He carried on going. Who were they? Police? If so, they'd quickly pieced it together that Sharny had worked there—she'd have definitely been found by now.

He should have checked the footage on his phone instead of coming here. He'd attached a small camera to lampposts at Kitchen Street and Debbie's Corner a while back and regularly seethed when he viewed the live feeds.

Now he seethed at being so stupid in coming here.

He drove to The Angel, the closest pub. He'd have breakfast, a breather. He parked out the front and got out, glancing over at the watcher in the alley, then at the girls on the corner. It was business as usual, although it seemed security had been upped as another man stood near the corner, leaning on the doorframe of The Roxy, hands in his pockets. Unless it was a punter, getting up the courage to approach one of the slags, Slasher would bet Debbie had erred on the side of caution and doubled the security. It didn't matter. He didn't need to come here to pick up the others on his list. He knew their movements, knew exactly where they'd be on their days off if they stuck to their usual routines.

Slasher—he liked thinking of himself as that— entered the pub and immediately spotted Lillibet. *She* spotted *him*, too, and her eyes widened in surprise. There was no way she could recognise him from last night, he'd had a balaclava on, but she *would* recognise him from work. So he didn't appear rude, he walked over to her and propped both elbows on the bar.

"Hello, stranger." He smiled. His heart did a little flutter. So she still had an effect on him in *that* way, then. Such a shame that his plans for their life together had been ruined by her choices. If only she hadn't decided to become a slag. "How have you been?"

"Getting by," she said.

He'd been so lost after she'd handed in her notice. He'd fancied her for the longest time but hadn't plucked up the courage to ask her out. She hadn't stated where she was going to go next, so he'd followed her. Finding out she'd chosen to sell herself on Kitchen rather than work for his family had infuriated him. Confused him. He'd already mapped out their lives: marriage, kids, a dog, all of it. Seeing her standing there, hip cocked, her clothes tarty, had been the push he'd needed, setting him off on this path. She'd given him the green light to murder. To prevent their imagined kids knowing their mother was a slapper.

He'd been contemplating killing prossers for years but had never taken that final step—until she'd touted her wares with that other dirty bitch who'd worked for his father. Pippa. Where was she now, though? She hadn't been on Kitchen for long after Lillibet had set up shop there. He'd convinced himself that she'd lured Lillibet to Kitchen, extolling the benefits, all that money they could earn, and she'd been the original slag at the top of his list so he could punish her for corrupting the woman he'd become obsessed with. But with Pippa vanishing, he'd chosen Lola, someone easily snatched, someone to practise on. Verity and Olivia had come next, and after that, he'd felt confident enough to go for Lillibet.

Except it had gone wrong and he'd had to grab Sharny.

"What have you been up to?" he asked.

"This and that. You?"

The bitch beside Lillibet, Debbie, poked her oar in. "Err, who are you?"

It's none of your business who I am. You should be ashamed of yourself, running women the way you do.

"It's fine, Deb." Lillibet wafted her hand around. "Billy's my ex-boss' son."

Debbie's shoulders relaxed, although she eyed Billy warily. "If you're sure... I'll just nip to the loo, then."

Lillibet nodded. "Yep, I'll be okay."

Debbie walked off through a double doorway.

"Why *wouldn't* you be fine?" Slasher frowned.

"Oh, it's nothing." Lillibet's face flushed.

"No, come on, tell me. I miss our chats whenever I went into the office. The place isn't the same without you."

She smiled. "It's just this Slasher business. It's got me on edge."

"Why are you even worried? He only goes for sex workers, so the papers say."

Her cheeks turned red. "I know, but…"

A lady approached behind the bar and made eye contact with him. "What can I get you?"

Slasher hid his irritation that she'd interrupted his alone time with Lillibet. "Err, a coffee and a full English, please, but no grilled tomato." He turned to Lillibet. "Can I get you anything?"

"Just a coffee for me and Deb, thanks."

He gritted his teeth. He didn't want to buy that Debbie tart a bloody coffee, but if he refused, it would look off. "Two more coffees, then." He took his card out as the barmaid went off to prod at the till. "Have you seen Pippa since she left Fords'?"

"A few times, but she's moved up north."

"I see. What are you up to these days? Sorry, I've already asked that, haven't I."

"Yes, and the answer is the same. This and that."

Was she ashamed of what she did? Was that why she'd avoided telling him what her job was?

Filthy cow. She could have been shacked up with me, treated like a princess, but she chose the wrong path.

The urge grew inside him, to grip her throat and squeeze.

The barmaid came back with a card reader, pulling him out of his thoughts. He tapped it to pay, annoyed Debbie returned and perched beside Lillibet again.

"We should go out," he said. "Catch up."

Debbie glowered at him. "No."

He raised his eyebrows, stunned she'd butted in on their conversation. "*Excuse* me?"

"I *said*, no."

Slasher challenged her with his glare. "What are you, her keeper?"

"Something like that."

Lillibet, flustered, put a hand on his wrist. "Maybe another time, just not at the minute. I've got things going on…"

Like hiding from me? He fought the need to chuckle. He must have really shit her up with that note. "Okay, well, here's my number for when you're ready." He took a business card from his wallet, handed it to her, then slipped his credit card away. "No pressure." He smiled at Debbie. "Nice to meet you." *It isn't.* "I'll see you around, Lillibet."

He wandered off to a nearby table, as close to them as he could get, but he was still too far away to hear any conversation. Debbie and Lillibet bent their heads together to talk, and the barmaid came over with his coffee.

He had a lot to think about, but the main thing running around his head was why he hadn't driven along Kitchen ages ago, made out he'd just happened to spot Lillibet there, and taken her off as a friend for a chat—then killed her. How *easy* it would have been. How dumb of him not to have gone down the obvious route.

He took his phone out, pretending to browse social media while he waited for his breakfast, glancing up every so often to check on Lillibet. She appeared deep in conversation, and it bugged him that she wasn't chatting to *him*, that he'd felt he had to move away and give her space.

One of the front doors opened, and alarm pierced him. That suited man and woman from Kitchen came in and walked straight up to

Debbie and Lillibet. They *had* to be the police. Was Lillibet going to be protected?

How am I meant to kill her now?

Chapter Eight

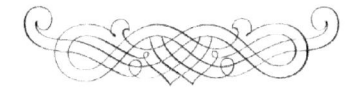

Billy knelt on the mat at the front door and stared out into the eyes in the letterbox opening. The stranger was here again, except he had a name now. Peter Ford. Peter had been coming here every night for weeks, but Billy had to keep it a secret. Mummy wouldn't be happy if she found out they talked. It was difficult for him to pretend, he didn't like lying to her, and he worried someone would see Peter speaking to

him where he crouched on the garden path. That would get him in trouble. Mummy would be cross.

"I have another little boy," Peter said. "His name is Darren, and he's six."

"But I'm your first boy?"

"Yes, you're my first boy."

"When can you take me bowling and to McDonald's?"

"I don't know, son. I need to ask your mummy to do something first."

"What's that?"

"It's a special test that will show you're mine."

"What, like the tests we have at school?"

"No, nothing like that." Peter sighed. "There's a thing called a swab, which takes a bit of spit out of your mouth, and I need Mummy to let me have it."

"I can let you have it." *Billy thought about the big house Peter had told him about, where there was a trampoline in the garden and a swimming pool. It sounded fun there, and he wanted to go and stay at weekends. Maybe go every day after school like Peter said so he didn't have to stay here alone. Mummy could pick him up when she'd finished work, although Peter said that soon, Billy could go and live there all the time.*

"I don't think that's a good idea," Peter said. "I'd rather your mummy knew about it. Do everything above board. There's been enough lies. It's all right. I'll contact my solicitor, and he'll sort it out for me."

"What's a solicitor?"

"There are a couple of meanings. Mummy is one of them because she solicits, but the other kind is a man or woman who do things for you, like helping you buy or sell a house, or get a divorce. Lots of things."

"Is that what Mummy does then? Helps people get divorced?"

"Um, no, her soliciting is entirely different. Remember what I told you, about the willies?"

Uncomfortable, Billy wanted to get up and run away. Peter said strange things sometimes, things Billy didn't understand, and because he loved his mummy, he had this weird feeling inside him that he was being naughty by letting Peter fill his head with all this stuff. That it was wrong.

"I'm going to bed now." Billy picked Mr Spencer up from the mat and stood, bending to peer through the letterbox. "See you tomorrow?"

"Yes, I'll be here."

Billy went upstairs, the letterbox flap snapping shut. In Mummy's bedroom, he looked down from the window. Peter got in his car, like he always did, where he stayed until Mummy got home. Peter had a wife, and she didn't mind him coming here every night. She wanted to meet Billy. And now he had a brother. What was Darren like? Did they look the same?

"I hope Mummy does the test," he said to Mr Spencer and wandered off to bed.

Mummy stared at the letter she'd opened. Tears fell down her red cheeks, and she swiped them away with the back of her shaking hand. Billy didn't like seeing her so upset. Was the letter from a neighbour? Did it say about Peter coming here every night?

"What's the matter?" he asked, clutching Mr Spencer.

She picked up a slim white box that had been in the padded envelope. "I...I'm going to need to put something in your mouth and send it off."

Billy frowned. "What?"

She put the letter down and tore open the box. It had two long cotton buds in it and some other things. "This. I just need some spit, okay?"

Excitement knotted in his tummy. This was the test? "How come you have to do that?"

"It's from your dad. He...he wants to know who you are."

"How come he didn't before?"

"I...um...I didn't tell him you were in my tummy."

"Why not?"

"He's...he's not a nice man."

Billy thought Peter was all right, apart from saying the stuff about willies and how Mummy was a bad lady for leaving him on his own. *"Why isn't he nice?"*

"I can't tell you that."

"Can I ask him myself?"

"No. I don't want you to have any contact with him."

"Why?"

"Because I'd prefer you didn't get influenced by him."

"Why?"

Mummy glared at him. *"Stop asking questions. Go and play. Let me think for a minute."*

Billy sat at the table with Mr Spencer. He didn't want to go away, he wanted to make sure she didn't put the box in the bin. Mummy read a little booklet that she'd taken out of it. She sighed and came over holding the bud.

"Open your mouth."

He did.

She scraped it against the inside of his cheek for what seemed like ages, then she took it back to the worktop.

"Right, that's that, then." She smiled, then muttered, "I'll need to go and see a solicitor. No way is he having anything to do with my son."

Billy wasn't sure if he'd heard her right. "What did you say, Mummy?"

"Nothing!"

"Why do you need a solicitor when that's what you are?"

"Pardon?"

"You're a solicitor, aren't you?"

"Who told you that?"

"No one." Billy had broken the golden rule. He'd spoken about something Peter had said. Would he be in trouble now? With Peter? All this secret-keeping was getting too much. His eyes prickled.

"Shall we go to the park?" Mummy did what she usually did when things got too big for her to cope with. She suggested fun times.

Billy nodded. He had big things to cope with, too, and going on the swings and roundabout would mean he'd forget them for a bit.

They set off, Billy clutching her hand, Mr Spencer in his other. Peter's car came down the street, but

Mummy didn't seem to see him until he stopped and opened his window.

"Emma, we need to talk."

She stopped, gasped, and shoved Billy behind her. "Go away. Leave us alone."

"Did you get the package and letter?"

"Yes."

"Are you going to send it in?"

"Yes, but you're not having access."

"That's for the court to decide, not you."

"I'm going to tell them everything."

"Really? You're going to admit what you do for a living, plus leaving your son on his own at night to do it? Good luck with that."

"Why are you being such an arsehole? Why come and find us now, all these years later?"

"Because you didn't tell me he existed at the time. You stopped seeing me, remember. I had to find out about him when I saw you both in town. He's the spitting image of my other son."

"So you're still with her, then?"

"Of course. Why would I divorce her when her father funded my business? I'd be a fool."

"I bet you're still sleeping around."

"That's no concern of yours."

"It is if my son is exposed to it."

Peter's laugh bellowed out. "You're such a hypocrite. Think about what you do with men, Emma. What you did with me, no condom, putting yourself at risk, possibly catching a disease. He's going to find everything out one day, and how will you explain that?"

"I do what I have to so I can feed him, pay the bills."

"Normal mothers work in supermarkets or something."

"You know why I can't do that."

"Oh yes, your conviction. Silly me for forgetting. Still, that's another black mark against you in court."

"Please, don't do this."

"I told you not to cross me, and you did. I warned you what would happen. How angry I get when people don't do as I say. Did you think it didn't apply to you anymore? Did you think that by changing where you stand at night that I wouldn't find you?"

"You hurt me."

"So? A bit of rough and tumble is okay."

"It was more than that, and you know it."

"In your line of work, a black eye or two is the norm."

"I should have reported you to the police for what you did."

"Hmm, but you'd already done six months for theft, and you were soliciting, for God's sake. Whereas I'm a business owner, respectable, married. Hmm, I wonder who they'd have believed? It would have been put down to another punter giving you a wallop."

Mummy turned and snatched Billy's hand. "Don't listen to him. Come on."

She stalked down the pavement, Billy running to keep up. All the things Peter had said twisted in his little mind, and he tried to make sense of them. What was a conviction? A condom? What was a spitting image? What was sleeping around? Had Peter hit Mummy? Was that why she'd said he was a bad man?

They walked for a while, then the grumble of an engine had her stiffening. Peter's car moved slowly beside them.

"This is harassment," she said. "Go away or I'll phone the police."

"Be my guest. Then I can tell them that for the past several weeks I've been outside your house every night because you've been leaving Billy by himself."

"How do you know his name?"

"I have my ways."

Billy had told him and, scared she'd guess, he looked up at his mother. Tears covered her cheeks, but she didn't wipe them away. She pushed on, her lips wobbling, and Billy felt horrible for lying to her. Should he tell her about Peter's visits, no matter that she'd get cross? But then Peter would be cross, too… Billy didn't know what to do, and worms wriggled in his belly, and it hurt.

"Remember, Emma, I know so much about you. You told me everything when you thought I loved you."

"Because I trusted you. That's why I agreed to no condom. I thought you were going to…"

"Yes, you fell for it and assumed I'd leave my wife. Silly girl. Women like you are just playthings, you're not destined for marriage or decent relationships. You're soiled, filthy, and only handy for a bit of fun."

Peter drove off, his tyres screeching, and Mummy flinched.

"How do you feel about moving away?" she asked.

"I like our house."

"But you said ghosts come and it scares you."

That was true, but…but if they moved, he wouldn't see Peter anymore.

"I want to stay where we are," he said.

"Then do a lot of praying, Billy, because Mummy's got a tough road ahead."

Chapter Nine

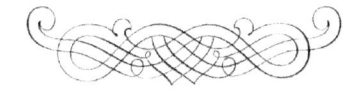

George and Greg stood at Frank Solloway's door once again. The day was nippy as eff, and it looked like it might rain. Dark clouds scudded overhead, and George would bet Frank wished he'd stayed in sunnier climes.

The man opened up, his face displaying his alarm, eyebrows lifted, his mouth dropping open. So his sister hadn't told him they'd been here during the night? George supposed that wasn't so unimaginable. It would have been the early hours by the time Frank had got through customs and whatnot. But hadn't she said she'd driven him to the airport? Had she driven him back, too?

"Err, can I help you?" Frank fiddled with his belt buckle, a brass affair in the shape of an old-fashioned cartwheel.

"Yeah, we need a word," George said. "Indoors."

Frank didn't hesitate. He stepped back and let them in. The front door opened directly into the living room, one with flowery furniture from the eighties, the carpet geometric, clashing. George's retinas were highly offended, and he winced. He sat on an armchair with doily-type things draped over the arms, crocheted as far as he could make out. Greg closed the door and remained there. Frank opted for the sofa.

"We're aware you've been away," George said. "Did your sister collect you from the airport?"

"Yeah…"

"Didn't she tell you we'd already been here?"

"No."

"Bit weird, isn't it, not mentioning The Brothers have been round?"

Frank shrugged. "She didn't get a word in edgeways. I was telling her all about my holiday."

"Got any proof of where you've been?"

Frank nodded. He grabbed his phone off the windowsill and prodded the screen. He moved closer, held it up, showing it to George. A holiday schedule from Tui. George studied it, making a mental note of the departure date.

"What's going on?" Frank sat again, on the edge of the seat, as if he wanted to be ready to bolt in case they did him over.

George hid a chuckle at the thought of him shitting himself. "Your number plate was clocked last night at the Plaza. Some geezer in a car thought a woman was touting for business. She declined, got in a taxi, and went home. But the bloke, he went to her house, had a balaclava on, and he dropped a note through the letterbox."

"It wasn't me!"

"I didn't say it was, did I?"

"No."

"So don't jump the gun. Anyway, the note implied the woman was next on his list—as in, he's the Slasher."

Frank used his cardigan sleeve to mop his brow. "Jesus. So he used my number plate? What did he do, take it off my motor then put it back?"

"No, he'd have had one made. Or someone used your car while you were away. Your sister said it hasn't moved, though."

"It wouldn't have done. I've got a steering wheel lock on it, and the key's on my keyring, and I took that on holiday with me as it's got the house keys on it an' all."

"Is there anyone who lives down here who's slim and short?"

"Only one bloke, and he's eighty."

"Any teens?"

"Nah, everyone down here is over fifty."

Satisfied they were definitely barking up the wrong tree, although George had to come here to be sure because he'd fucked up in the past, he stood. "Cheers for your time. Keep this little natter under your hat. The police know about the plate, and they won't want that info getting out. You'll probably get a visit from them to check your alibi."

"Right." Frank got up. "I saw on the news earlier another poor cow copped it. Was it the woman you said about?"

"No, someone else."

"Bless her. I use a few girls on Kitchen. Do you know which one it was?"

"Yeah, but the police haven't released that information yet, so I'm not going to. Fond of the women there, are you?"

"Yep. They've made me feel less lonely since my wife died."

"When was that?"

"Two years ago."

George glanced around. "Did the missus decorate this room?"

"Um, yes?"

"Maybe change it. Having reminders of her in your face might be what's making you miss her more."

Frank sighed. "I know that, but I've been putting it off."

George nodded. "Word of advice. I'd keep away from Kitchen for a bit if I were you. You'll be seen cruising. The police will likely be there on and off."

"Oh, okay. Thanks."

"We'll see ourselves out."

Back in the car, George turned to Greg. "I'm pissed off I didn't check his car last night. I'd have seen the steering wheel lock."

"You were too arsey to think straight."

"Hmm." George thought about what they could do next. "We'll nip and see Bennett. He deals with the CCTV near Kitchen and the Plaza."

"Janine will already be dealing with that."

"Yeah, I know, but I want to see shit for myself. And the pigs could take ages to trawl through it."

"Fair enough."

George drove to Bennett's place of work and tapped on the office door.

Bennett opened it and glanced back over his shoulder, then looked at George. "There's two of us today," he whispered.

"So?" George patted his suit front where his interior pocket was. "I've got enough cash on me."

"Jones isn't the type to take a bribe or do anything he shouldn't. Bit of a do-gooder."

"I'll have to change his mind then, won't I."

"Bloody hell," Bennett mumbled and let them in.

"All right?" George asked the nerdy blond man sitting in front of a bank of monitors.

Thick-lensed glasses enlarged Jones' eyes, and his strange little moustache had paedo vibes about it. George told himself that not everyone who had a moustache was a pervert, but still, he couldn't get it out of his head now he'd thought it.

Jones stared from George to Greg to Bennett. "Um, no one's allowed in here."

George smiled. "I know. Your colleague knows an' all, but I just threatened to kneecap him if he didn't let us in. I've got a favour to ask — and you *will* grant it."

"What kind of favour?" Jones stuttered.

"The kind where you find a number plate for me on a car that was out last night. The kind where you get a grand in your little mitts and no one says a thing about it."

"I…I can't. I'd lose my job."

"How? No one but us four will know."

Jones shook his head. "No, I can't risk it."

"What, you need this job that badly?"

"Yeah, I've got four kids."

"Then you could do with a grand, couldn't you? I mean, that sort of cash would help you out, wouldn't it?"

"Yes, but—"

"If you don't find me the information I want, sunshine, I'll break your fucking neck, and then you'll be dead at worst or paralysed at best. *Then* what will your kids do, eh?"

"Just do it," Bennett said. "This is The Brothers we're dealing with here."

"Oh God… I didn't…I'm sorry, I didn't know. I haven't lived here long."

George smiled. "Well, now you *do* know, so get those fingers of yours working on that keyboard before I lose my shit." He found the number plate on their phone and recited it. "Chop-chop." He turned to Bennett. "Be a love and make us a brew, will you?"

Bennett smirked, and George winked, happy that Bennett had played the game well. The kettle boiled quickly, so these two must have not long had a cuppa. Bennett made the drinks while Jones breathed heavily, likely in a panic. He clicked on the mouse and searched the hits that had come up on the screen.

"Okay," Jones said, "it's been to a fair few places."

"What are they?" George asked.

Jones listed them. The Plaza was there, as was a road with shop CCTV close to Kitchen. So the tosser had had the balls to drive to the source and collect Sharny. Of all the brass neck.

"That's all I needed to know." George took two envelopes out of his pocket and threw them on the desk. "One each."

Bennett handed out the teas, and they stood drinking in silence, Bennett acting like he didn't know what to do with himself, Jones staring at his desk as if he didn't dare look anywhere else.

"It's pretty simple, mate," George said. "No need to crap your kecks. I wanted information, you gave it. You pop that envelope in your coat pocket and we say no more about it. If you *do* blurt it out, though, we'll come back and I'll do what I promised. Think of your kids, that's the sensible thing to do."

Jones nodded.

"Bloody cold weather, isn't it," George said.

"Y-yes," Jones muttered.

"Christmas is around the corner."

Jones rubbed shaking hands down his face.

George shouldn't be fucking with him by chatting shit, the bloke had done them a solid, albeit under duress, so he decided to be nice. "What kind of things do your kids want from Father Christmas?"

Jones seemed on the verge of crying. "A PlayStation for the b-boys, and the g-girls want iPhones."

"Blimey, kids today, they don't want much, do they? When *we* were kids, we were chuffed to get pyjamas and a book. Where do you live?"

Jones snapped his gaze to George. "What?"

"Come on, I know you're not deaf. Where do you live? If you don't tell me, I'll find out anyway."

"Twenty-four Globe Road."

"Does your wife have a job? If you even have a missus."

"Um, she works from home."

"Good, then she'll be there when one of our men drop the presents round, won't she."

Jones nodded. "She'll ask me questions. What will I say?"

"Dunno, but I'm sure you'll figure it out. Say you got a cash bonus. See, people who do things for us get looked after. Now I know you're such a receptive chap, we'll use you more often."

"Oh God…"

George gulped some tea. "Calm your tits. You'll get used to it." He drank a bit more and, as it was too hot to finish, he handed his cup to Bennett. "Pleasure doing business with you."

He led the way out of the building.

Greg grumbled behind him. "I didn't get a chance to finish my sodding tea."

"Stop whinging, you fanny. I need to ring Janine and let her know where that car's been."

They got in the BMW, and George gave her a bell on speaker, listing all the locations.

"That doesn't help me," she said. "I can't say anything because people will wonder why I got the info when it hasn't come to me via the proper channels."

"I just thought it'd give you a head start for when it *does* come in. Fuck me, talk about ungrateful."

"Right, well, thank you."

"You're bloody welcome." He ended the call and leaned his head back. "She can be a right mardy cow sometimes, more so lately."

"I've told you before, she's not approachable when she's up against it. She's walking a dodgy line when we're involved in her investigations. She's got to keep her head in the game so she doesn't slip up—so *we* don't get caught."

"And *I've* told *you* before, she knew what she was walking into with us, so I don't care."

"What, even though you know what she's been through as Victim C?"

George thought about that. Janine, known as Rusty back then, had been held captive in a basement flat in her late teens, raped, abused, her mind fucked over. The people who'd held her had tried to get her pregnant so they could steal the baby. It had explained why she was so brusque, how she didn't suffer fools gladly. When they'd first met her, she'd been rude and abrasive towards them, and it had grated on George. She was still rude, but they'd got used to it, and once her story had come out, he'd totally understood her behaviour.

Shit, yeah, he felt sorry for her regarding that. She'd recently been seeing a female therapist to get her head straight, and she'd shacked up officially with Cameron, a bodyguard they'd assigned to her so she was kept safe, but like he'd said to Greg, she'd known what she was getting into with them, she'd agreed to everything, and it was her *job* to cope with making sure she didn't slip up.

"All right, I'll go easier on her." *If I feel like it.* George drove away.

"How long before you forget you said that and you come down hard on her again?"

"Ah, give it a bloody rest, will you?"

"No. You need telling sometimes. You get tunnel vision and don't put yourself in someone else's shoes often enough."

"So you said with Lillibet." He didn't want to talk about this anymore. "I'm hungry, so we'll stop for food."

"Deflecting, as usual." Greg sighed. "Shall I ring Nessa to get her to have your Pot Noodle ready for when we walk in?"

"Yeah." George's stomach rumbled.

"Serves you right for not eating breakfast," Greg said, all smug.

"You made me muesli, so what did you expect?"

"We need to eat healthier, my doctor said."

"*You* can eat healthy, but I'm not. You can stick that rabbit food up your jacksy."

Greg sighed again. "There's no telling you, is there?"

George smiled. "Nope."

Chapter Ten

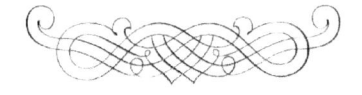

Lillibet had given Janine her version of what had happened last night, and now they were back on Kitchen Street. The other women seemed uneasy with Debbie being there, as if they thought she was watching them to pick fault. She wasn't, she fitted in well and chatted to everyone like they were old mates. Still, no one liked the boss hanging around, did they.

Nervous, Lillibet stamped her numb, cold feet, worried in case a punter stopped and specifically asked for her. It had been dark last night when she'd seen the Slasher's eyes as he'd peered out at her through the gap at the top of his car window, and she didn't think she'd recognise them if he spoke to her today. It bothered her that she'd have no idea whether it was the killer or not. Then there was tonight to get through. And her being here now was stupid, wasn't it? It was meant to be her second day off, so if the Slasher had been watching, he'd know her patterns and wonder why she was at work, wouldn't he?

Her phone rang, and she checked the screen, surprised Billy's name showed up. She had his number programmed in her mobile from when she'd worked for his dad and had thought it odd that he'd given her his business card earlier. She showed Debbie the screen.

"Answer it, but fob him off if he's after a date again," Debbie said. "And put it on speaker so I can hear what he's saying. There's something off about him. I can't put my finger on it, but I bet he's got some murky shit in his past. He reminds me of one of those old-fashioned flashers, know the kind I mean?"

"The ones in beige macs?"

"Yes!"

Lillibet smiled and swiped the screen. "Hello?"

"It's me, Billy."

"I know."

"Oh." He sounded stumped. "Err, *how* did you know that?"

She faked a chuckle. "I've still got your number from Fords', so it came up on my phone."

"Ah, right." He laughed—well, it was more of a manic giggle.

Debbie stared at the phone in shock and mouthed, "Creepy much?"

Lillibet bit her lip. Debbie's reaction was funny, but she was right, the giggle *was* creepy. He used to laugh like that around Lillibet a lot, and all the women at work had thought he was someone to be avoided. Thank God he hadn't come in much.

"Where are you?" he asked.

Her stomach muscles tensed. That was as bad as being asked what she was wearing. It felt sinister, or maybe her nerves were so taut she was being silly. "Why?"

"Just wondered if you fancied a spot of early lunch. I've been thinking about you all morning. Sorry, that sounded wrong. What I meant was, bumping into you meant I thought about you. Not in a perverted way or anything, just... I should shut up really. I'm digging a deeper hole with everything I'm saying."

Debbie shook her head, annoyed, and whispered, "Tell him to piss off."

Lillibet wanted to end the call instead but was too polite to cut him off like that. It wasn't his fault she found him weird. Plus, in The Angel, she hadn't had the guts to say she didn't want to go out with him and had said something like, 'Maybe another time', so it was her fault he was asking again.

What could she say to put him off? "I'm at work."

"Really?"

Why did he say that?

Lillibet swallowed. "Hang on, two secs." She put it on mute. "He's giving me the willies."

"Definite red flag," Debbie said. "It sounded like he was surprised you're at work. Why? It's a weekday, so it's a given where you'd be. You don't think it could be him, do you?"

"Billy? The Slasher? No! He's odd and always stared at me funny, but he wouldn't be the killer."

"He's the right height and build…"

A shiver raced through Lillibet. "Bloody hell, Deb…"

"Get rid of him. Now."

Lillibet took mute off. "Sorry about that. I have to go."

"What is it you're doing for work now?" he asked as if her needs didn't matter. Pushy. Annoying.

"The same thing as at Fords'."

"Hmm, strange. I don't recall us having to send out any references for you."

Why would that even have stuck in his mind? Why would he even know that when he barely did anything at the office? Had he gone and *checked*? Why?

Irritation ploughed into her at him giving her a grilling. "That's because I didn't need any. Look, thanks for the lunch offer, but I'm busy."

A car swept past.

"It sounds like you're outside," he said.

She gritted her teeth. "I am."

"How peculiar, when your type of job is in an office. Are you sitting by an open window by any chance?"

"I'm on a break with a colleague." *Why am I explaining myself?*

"*Are* you now. Is she a smoker, then?"

"Um, yes. I really do have to go."

"Okay, what about going out tonight instead? Your bulldog was in attack mode earlier and put a block on us having a date. Now she's not there, you can speak for yourself."

"I *am* here," Debbie said, "and the answer's still the same. Fuck off."

Lillibet stabbed the END button and stuffed the phone in her pocket. She wanted to laugh and cry at the same time. Was she getting herself all confused? Had she felt bad vibes from Billy because she had the Slasher business on her mind? If it was a different situation, would she have felt he was being pushy or just that he was eager to have a date with her?

Debbie drew in a sharp breath. "You've got a possible stalker on your hands. I bet he fancied you when you worked at Fords' and he didn't have the balls to ask you out. He seems that sort."

"I did get the feeling he liked me but I brushed it off. He was barely in the office. If he fancied me, wouldn't he have come in more? Anyway, he isn't my type."

"Well, you're his. Is he married or anything?"

"Not that I'm aware of."

"That figures. Who'd bloody have him? Honestly, he's off, there's something not right there."

"Should I let The Brothers know about him just in case?" Somehow, and curiously, the idea that Billy was the Slasher made Lillibet feel better. Because she knew him, the killer didn't seem so scary now. But what if it *wasn't* him? The twins might hurt him for no reason, and all because she and Debbie thought he was weird?

Debbie nodded. "Probably better to be safe than sorry. They can look into him or get Janine to."

Lillibet composed a message to them and pressed SEND. "Done."

She spent the rest of the afternoon creeped out and wishing she could go home. And it felt wrong, telling punters she didn't want to go with them when they asked for her. This could ruin her rep, one she'd built up carefully. When she returned to work properly after this was all over, they might not approach her because she'd rejected them today. Men and their bruised egos…

She wished she hadn't agreed to do this. But what George had said floated through her mind, and he was right. If she was bait and they caught the Slasher, it meant no one else died.

But it doesn't mean I won't.

That thought almost sent her running, so she linked her arm through Debbie's and took comfort from their closeness. "Is it me, or do you feel like we're being watched?"

Debbie glanced up and down the street. "It's not just you, but maybe that's because the killer must have been keeping tabs on girls and we know that, so it's affecting us. No one's in any cars down here, so unless he's like Crook with a telescope or he lives in one of these houses…"

Lillibet sighed. "I just want today to be over."

"I know, love. Don't worry, you'll be all right. This time tomorrow, the Slasher will be dead if he approaches you tonight."

Lillibet clung to that thought. She'd have a third death on her hands. Stephanie, Sharny, and the Slasher. Three names beginning with S. She didn't know whether to be freaked out by *that* as well.

Pack it in. Calm down.

Easier said than done.

Chapter Eleven

Annoyed she'd lied to him, Slasher sat in a Vauxhall down a side street and brooded, the engine running so he could have the heat on. He'd checked the camera feed on his phone before he'd rung her and knew damn well she stood on Kitchen with Debbie. Yes, she'd been truthful when she'd said she was at work—*why was she there today anyway?*—but she'd bullshitted him about doing the same job as she had at Fords'. It was clear she didn't want him to know she was a slag, and he couldn't blame her, not with how people felt about it, but it reminded him of his mother, the deception. It fuelled his need to kill Lillibet, and the burn of it raced through him, hot and heady. He rested his head back and closed his eyes to get it under control.

Once he'd regained some inner peace, he opened his eyes. He must have fallen asleep without realising. Darkness cloaked the street, punctuated by the orange glows from lampposts. A light fog had descended, which pissed him off. Like he could do with that hampering his progress tonight, although it might do him a favour. Less chance of people seeing him.

He glanced at the clock on the dash. Five-forty. Shit, Lillibet finished work at half five, and he was supposed to have followed her taxi home. He snatched his phone off his lap and accessed the feed for Kitchen. She stood with Debbie and a few other women, chatting. Relief punched him in the gut that he hadn't missed her. He drove to the next street beside Kitchen. Checked the feed again. Lillibet and Debbie were walking away, arms linked. Why hadn't a taxi arrived? He'd done his homework, and Debbie paid for all the women to go home in one.

Were they going to The Angel, seeing as it wasn't far away?

He debated whether to get out and follow them on foot or go straight to Lillibet's house. He opted for the latter and drove there, parking down the road so he wasn't seen but he could see the property. Why was one of the downstairs lights on? Had she forgotten to turn it off before she'd gone to work?

A tense thirty minutes later and a black cab pulled up to the kerb. She got out—but so did Debbie. God, was she having dinner there or something? Or were they going out tonight and they planned to get glammed up together?

This would complicate things. What if Debbie was staying over? He wouldn't be able to get Lillibet alone. No, Debbie only had a handbag, a big one that could hold the clothes she might be changing into if they *were* going on the lash.

The women went inside, and the hallway light snapped on.

In the rearview, another vehicle caught his attention, fog swirling in the headlamps' beams. The car swerved into a space between two others, but the driver didn't get out. Was this surveillance provided by The Brothers? The police? Lillibet *must* have told them about him being here last night and posting that note. Or maybe it was a man coming home from work but he couldn't bear to go inside yet. He could have a nagging wife and umpteen kids he had to brace himself to face. Whatever, Slasher didn't like it. Should he drive away? Leave Lillibet for now and select one of the others on Debbie's Corner to get rid of the urge that kept pecking at him? But there were two men watching the corner now, more chance of him being spotted. He wished he'd bought a fake beard or at least a moustache. A wig.

To pass the time—and he wondered whether Lillibet and Debbie would stay in tonight, leaving him sitting here for hours—he ordered a beard and wig from Amazon then brought up Uber Eats. He'd get his dinner delivered to his car. McDonald's on the way, he sat and stared into the rearview mirror, only the side of the other driver's face visible. Whoever it was must be browsing his phone, as a slight glow lit up the skin above his beard and reflected in the lens of his black-framed glasses. Not knowing who he was irritated the shit out of him, and he gritted his teeth. If he got out and asked questions, it'd draw attention to himself. He wasn't stupid enough to do that, but bloody hell, he wanted to.

What would Dad do?

Slasher thought back to when Peter, as he'd called him then, had spoken to Mum that day they'd gone to the park. He'd been self-assured in his fancy car, stated how he'd felt, no messing. That conversation had puzzled Slasher for a long time afterwards, and he hadn't known the full truth until much later, when Dad had explained everything to him.

"She lied to everyone, son. She was a bit of a cow as a teen, acting up, shoplifting, and generally being a nuisance. She progressed from nicking in shops to robbing a petrol station." Dad sighed. "I know, I know, not what you expected to hear. Anyway, she got caught. She didn't have a weapon on her, and she'd been under eighteen, so she spent time in a young offender's place. By then, her parents hadn't wanted anything to do with her, and when she was let out, she was put in a bedsit and claimed benefits."

Billy tried to imagine Mum being that sort of person but failed. "Is this a joke?"

"Afraid not. Two months after getting out, she was walking the streets and selling her body. Three years later, she met me. I explained I was married to Michaela. Your mother had, quite wrongly, assumed I'd leave my wife for her. It was my fault. I told her I loved her, but I had no intention of breaking up my marriage."

"So why go with Mum if you were with Michaela? I don't get it."

"You're a man now. You have urges, yes? Michaela, she's…look, talking to your dad about sex is a bit off, but your mum was different, gave me something I needed, something Michaela won't provide."

"Right."

"I'll admit I hit Emma. I regret it—I was young and stupid, couldn't control my emotions."

Slasher understood how that felt. Dad's relationship with Mum had been a powder keg waiting to go up from the start, and Dad had severed contact with her when he'd realised she wasn't to be trusted: she'd threatened to tell Michaela everything, so of course he'd binned her off.

The fact she was pregnant at the time, well, she'd kept that to herself.

"She hid it from me, Billy. I mean, who does that? You know how much money I've got, how I could have made your life better, yet she chose to flaunt herself to make cash instead. There wasn't any need, I would have been there for you. If I'm honest, had I known she was pregnant, I'd have applied for custody as soon as you were born. Her life, what she was doing… You know all about it now, and it wasn't good, was it?"

Billy shook his head. "No."

Since living with Dad, Michaela, and Darren, Billy had been told so many things over the years that he hadn't known about Mum. What he still struggled with, though, was how the picture Dad painted didn't match the mother he'd known. Yes, she'd left him on his own at night, but she'd been good to him, always making sure he had food, and love, and cuddles. She wasn't this monster Dad made her out to be.

"She wasn't all bad," Billy said.

"No, she brought you up to look after yourself, so she did something right, but the things you've done since coming to live with us… She failed on that. I keep telling you there's no reason to act out, but you do it anyway."

"You can't blame her entirely. You didn't wear a condom. Knowing what she did for a living… You put Michaela at risk. VD or whatever."

"Like I said, I was young and stupid."

That was twice Dad had said that. If he was allowed to be young and stupid and still turn out a good bloke, why wasn't Mum given the same privilege?

Billy battled with his warring emotions, something he'd done ever since he'd been taken in by social services after—

He refused to think of that night. It never did him any good.

Slasher had always known he'd had a dad. Mum had said he didn't live with them because he had another family, that he wasn't a nice man. Why had she chosen the day of the park to really drive it home, to say what she had to his father in front of Slasher? Likely because she'd known the net was closing in. Peter had wanted to claim Slasher as his with that test, and she must have realised he'd put his side of events forward, so she'd wanted to taint Slasher's view of him, perhaps so he'd refuse to have anything to do with him.

Jolted out of his trip down Memory Lane by a tap on the window, he cursed himself for once again forgetting to remain alert. A man in a black bike helmet, the visor up, stared at him holding up a McDonalds' bag. Slasher wound his window down and accepted his dinner. He nodded to the Uber bloke and put the window back up but left a slight gap so the heat from the food didn't create too much steam on the glass. He needed to be able to see out, although the light fog was still around.

The driver sped off on his moped. Slasher munched on his Big Mac and watched Lillibet's house. A bedroom light came on, and two human-shaped shadows stood behind the thin, closed curtains, facing each other as if the people chatted. One head bent, and an arm came up, a hand resting on a shoulder. Debbie consoling Lillibet about receiving the note? About having to involve the police?

Slasher smiled at Lillibet's upset. Ate a few chips. Finished his burger.

If they were in the bedroom, *surely* they were getting ready to go out.

He nodded to himself. As the plans may have to change and he might not be able to approach Lillibet as she waited for a taxi later, he'd see where they went and gauge the situation. If it looked like he could plausibly 'bump' into her, he could perhaps persuade her, out of Debbie's earshot, to go with him.

What excuse could he used to lure her out to his car, though?

Chapter Twelve

Billy jumped at the sound of hard banging on the front door. Mummy was at work, and he'd been expecting Peter, but Peter didn't usually knock, he called through the letterbox. Was it someone else? Or was it one of the ghosts again?

Heart tripping, he grabbed Mr Spencer off the worktop and crept from the light and warmth of the oven to the kitchen doorframe. He waited for the letterbox flap to flip up, for fingers and eyes to appear, but nothing happened. Someone was out there, though. Their shape filled one of the panels in the door, although because of the wavy shapes in the glass, he couldn't see who it was.

Another shape loomed up beside it, and Billy whimpered.

"Who the fuck are you?" Peter said.

Relieved, Billy stepped closer to the front door, keeping his back to the wall near the living room.

"Who the fuck are you*?" another man said.*

Billy scooted across the hallway to the right to sit on the bottom of the stairs.

"Answer me first," Peter said.

"Look, I need to speak to Emma, all right? And what's it got to do with you anyway?"

"I'm her friend, so it has everything to do with me."

"What are you really, her pimp?"

What was a pimp?

Peter continued, "Fuck off. What do you want her for?"

"Not that I should have to explain myself to you, but I accidentally gave her a fifty-quid note last night, an extra one, two were stuck together. I need it back else my missus will go ape."

"Tough. And how the fuck did you know where she lives? Is she doing business from here now or what?"

"Nah, I followed her once."

"You did what*?"*

"You heard."

Peter's shadow lifted an arm, and a thud sounded. The second shadow staggered back, probably into the hedge that ran beside the garden path, and the grunting noises seemed so loud. Were they fighting? Billy scrunched his eyes shut, his chest hurting where it had gone all tight. When he opened them again, only one shadow remained. The letterbox flap opened, and eyes appeared. Billy couldn't make out if they were Peter's from this angle.

"Billy? You all right?"

Billy shot up and went to the door. It was okay if it was Peter. He gripped Mr Spencer hard, trying not to cry. "Who was that?"

"No one to worry about. He's gone now. Listen, Mummy didn't send the test off like she said she would, so she lied to me again. Can you let me in so I can talk to her when she gets home?"

Billy shook his head. "No, she'll get upset if I do that."

"Fair enough. What have you been doing today?"

"I went to school and stuff. We had a drawing competition."

"What did you draw?"

The image popped into Billy's mind. "You. And your house. The swimming pool. Miss put it on the wall in the classroom. She said it was really good."

"You can come and swim at mine one day, I promise."

Billy's heart leapt. "With Darren?"

"Yes, with Darren. And me and Michaela. We've got blow-up floats and a slide."

"Can Mummy swim in it?"

"I don't think she'd like that."

"But she loves swimming."

"Things are complicated when you're an adult. I assure you, Mummy wouldn't want to swim at my house. So, what else did you do?"

Billy thought about it. "At playtime, I kicked a ball about with Ollie."

"Ah, right. And what about when you came home?"

"Mummy did a jigsaw with me, then she tickled me until I peed myself."

"Tickled you? Was it fun?"

"Yeah."

"Where did she tickle you?"

"On my belly." Where else would it be?

"So not anywhere else?"

"No."

"It's just…sometimes big people tickle where they shouldn't, and if Mummy's doing that, I need to know because it means you're not safe. I'd have to tell the police about it, then you'd have to come and live with me."

Billy's tummy rolled over. *"But she doesn't do it anywhere else."*

"Oh."

Why did Peter sound like he wanted to get Mummy in trouble? Tears burned Billy's eyes, and he blinked to make them go away.

"Are you all right?" Peter asked.

"Yeah."

"Are you crying?"

"No."

"It looks like you are. Is it because you're telling me fibs and Mummy does *tickle you somewhere else?"*

"Stop it!"

Billy ran upstairs and flung himself on his bed. He stared at Mr Spencer in the dark and wished he *was a soldier like him. He'd shoot everyone who upset him, even Peter. But then he wouldn't be able to go swimming…*

Did he want to go and live with Peter if he got the police to take Mummy away? Yes, he'd go there, but he'd like it better if he could stay here and just go to Peter's at the weekend or when Mummy worked. It would be weird not being in this house. He couldn't remember living anywhere else.

He closed his eyes, tears spilling. He hated being confused after Peter had said stuff. Everything had been okay until he'd started talking to him. Well, okay apart from being left on his own, but he'd got through it every night, and Mummy always came in when she got back and shook him awake to let him know she was there, and she kissed his head and told him to have sweet dreams, my prince.

He cried himself to sleep.

Billy woke and stared at the ceiling. The floor creaked out on the landing, so Mummy must be home. He smiled and waited for her to come in, but she didn't. He listened. The floor in her room creaked, too, like it always did whenever he stepped inside, so Mummy must have just gone in there. Maybe she'd come and kiss him in a minute. She might be putting her handbag away in the locked drawer so if anyone came in to steal things, they wouldn't be able to take her wages.

When she still hadn't come in after a while, Billy's eyes drifted. He reckoned he'd imagined the creaking, or it was the ghosts, so he let himself go back to sleep. But he woke again, and whatever had pulled him out of his dream about Mr Spencer standing outside Buckingham Palace had him sitting upright. His heartbeat went all silly, like it had forgotten how to pulse, and he struggled to breathe properly.

Someone said, "Please, no…"

Mummy?

Billy shot out of bed, still clutching Mr Spencer, and ran to her door. It was closed except for a small gap, and he peered in. The bed under the window stood in view to the right, a lamp on, and she lay there, a man in black sitting on her, his head black, too, facing away from Billy. Where were her hands? Why wasn't she trying to push him away? Ah, the man's knees were on top of them, and he had his hands around her throat.

Billy slapped a palm over his mouth, something telling him to keep quiet and that if Mr Black saw him, there'd be trouble. It scared him that the man did the same, except one hand left her neck and went over Mummy's lips.

"Quiet. No need to make a fuss, is there?" Mr Black said.

Mum made a snuffling sound.

"You were asked to do one little thing, and you just couldn't do it, could you?" Mr Black leaned down so their faces were close. "This is the result."

He pulled something from his pocket and stuffed it in Mummy's mouth. A bright-yellow cloth, like the ones she used to clean the kitchen worktops with. Mr Black squeezed her throat with both hands, and Mummy made a horrible noise. He let her go, squeezed, let her go, all the while that noise coming out of her. He released her, flexing his fingers.

Mr Black took something else out of his pocket. A knife. He held it up, and Mummy struggled, trying to buck him off.

"No point fighting. You're not going anywhere. Now then, I've got to put a couple of things on you. Don't shoot the messenger, I just do what I'm paid to do. It's going to sting."

Mr Black put the tip of the knife under the front of Mummy's bra and cut it. He snatched the material to the sides. Billy had seen Mummy's boobies before when she'd had a bath with him, and it didn't bother him normally, but it did now. Mr Black showing them off, it seemed wrong. Was he going to put his willy inside her like Peter had said?

Where would he put it?

Mr Black groaned, and the wind chimes tinkled. Billy stared. Mr Black gripped Mummy's chin to hold her head still and drew something on her cheeks with the knife. Lots of blood came out, and Mummy cried, screeching sometimes. Billy wanted to shout at him to stop, but if he did that, the man might come after him.

"Okay, this X is a kiss from who wants you dead—maybe they still love you, I dunno. The Y is 'why?' Why did you lie? Why did you keep the secret? I was instructed to tell you that. Don't ask me what it's about, I wasn't told, but I suspect you know, otherwise I wouldn't have been asked to say it, would I."

A weird screech came out of Mummy around the cloth.

Mr Black laughed to himself then stabbed at the boobs. Then he cut her nipples, creating the plus signs Billy used in maths, and he wrote something on her chest, and it took ages. What did the words say?

Billy couldn't see because of the blood which ran down into her armpits. Mummy sobbed, and her cheeks…the blade must have gone right through because some of the skin flapped. That must be really painful.

Mr Black stabbed the knife into the side of her neck, the handle poking out. Mummy let out a horrible noise, and her eyes bulged. She lifted her head and her back a bit, then flopped down. Billy wanted to scream, to run at Mr Black and hurt him, but he couldn't move or make a sound. He was stuck there, staring, trying to understand what he was seeing. Mummy caught sight of him, and she shook her head from side to side as if to tell him no, he shouldn't be there. Billy couldn't look away from her eyes — they were so big and round, tears coming out of them.

Mr Black wrenched the knife out. Billy had never seen so much blood. It was like when Mummy squirted Fairy liquid into the sink when she was washing up. It shot out in spurts, landing on her pillow and quilt, staining it red. Her eyes closed.

Fear funnelled through Billy, and he wet himself. He tiptoed into the bathroom, avoiding the creaking area of the floor, and stood Mr Spencer on the top of the toilet cistern quietly. He took his pyjama bottoms off and put them in the sink, and again, something told him not to wash his legs, not to make any noise, so he grabbed Mr Spencer and went back to Mummy's door.

Mr Black had moved down and sat on her legs. He drew something on her belly with the knife, but Billy couldn't see what it was. The blood had stopped spurting out of her neck and just dribbled. Had all of it come out of her body? Was there nothing left? He stared at her tummy—some was coming out of the cuts there but not as much as it had on her chest.

Mr Black moved down even more and stabbed Mummy's private parts. Billy whimpered. The man stopped, knife held up. He turned his head to the side.

One eye inside a hole of a head mask. The glimpse of a mouth.

Billy held his breath.

"Who's there?" Mr Black said.

Frightened, Billy edged away from the door and stood in front of the airing cupboard. Mr Spencer in his hand, he looked down at him in the dim light coming from Mummy's room and, in his head, asked him what he should do. He pretended the soldier told him to go back to bed, so he crept there, getting under the covers and snapping his eyes shut, holding the soldier tight.

The blood and Mummy's sores filled his head. He tried to get them out, but they wouldn't go until he asked himself some questions. Did Mr Black know Billy was at home? Had he seen him in bed when he'd walked upstairs? And how come Mummy hadn't given Billy a kiss before she'd gone into her room? Was she going to do it after Mr Black had gone? Would she be able to without any blood inside her? Or would she come to see him in the morning? He hoped Mr Black put cream and plasters on those cuts like Mummy did for Billy when he fell over and hurt himself.

He cried, confused about what he'd seen—he knew it wasn't right to cut someone, so why hadn't he gone downstairs to phone the police? Why had he just stood and watched? He didn't understand himself and felt bad for not getting help, but that little voice answered his worries: If you'd done that, Mr Black would have cut you, too.

Would he still do that? Barge in here after he'd finished with Mummy?

Billy reckoned if he stayed really, really still, he'd be okay.

Mr Spencer agreed.

Chapter Thirteen

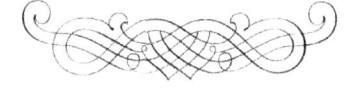

George had rung Janine to say a certain man might be of interest, something Lillibet had passed on to the twins. At the station in her office, Janine looked into Billy Ford—except he hadn't always been called that. Formerly Billy Meyers, he came up in a search that alarmed the shit out of her. He'd witnessed his mother's murder, although he hadn't spoken about it until a year and one week after her death. Apparently, he'd been mute for a month, then had talked about anything other than the murder until he'd finally found the courage to tell officers what he'd seen.

DI Zeller, now retired, and that ponce, Rod Clarke, had worked on the case. She was so annoyed that the paperwork wasn't as specific as hers was with investigations. As was the norm in day-to-day policing, the database was always checked to see if any murders matched those that were currently being worked on, yet this one hadn't come up during a previous search. But it *should* have done had it been filed correctly.

It mentioned 'wording' on the chest but not what those words were, the stabs to the breasts, and that a 'symbolic image' had been carved into the victim's skin but not what it was or where it was. A yellow cloth had been in her mouth. The case on the screen in front of her hadn't been flagged up because she'd put in specific keywords while hoping for a hit: lying, bitch, snake, carotid artery stab, X, Y.

It was obvious to Janine that Emma Meyers' case could well be linked to the Slasher investigation, and if the hit *had* come up, they might have caught him well before now. Lola Jennings would still have lost her life, as she was the first death to alert them that a murderer was around, but Verity Smith and Olivia Lock might have been saved.

But Billy had only been eight when his mother had died, and Janine couldn't believe a kid would have had the strength to hold his mum down while he cut into her. He could have tied her up while she'd slept, but there were no mention of ligature marks. The slices to her chest and breasts had been done while she was alive, according to the PM report, so she'd have been well able to fend an eight-year-old off. The stabs to the vagina and the 'symbolic image', suspected to have been administered after death, had question marks beside them as if the pathologist wasn't sure on that—perhaps due to the blood being wiped off the stomach, as if the killer had wanted the image to be seen clearly straight away?

I bet it was a serpent.

She read on. A man had been seen crouching outside Emma's house in the evenings for weeks prior to the murder, speaking through the letterbox. As Emma had been at work, it could only have been Billy he'd chatted with. The night of the murder, the killer had entered the home without breaking any windows or damaging the front door, so he'd either had a key, used a lock pick, or Emma had let him in. Billy had been in bed and had heard the floor creaking. He'd assumed it was his mother and had gone towards her bedroom to check.

Janine continued scanning the text, saddened that a child had seen such a horrible thing. No wonder he'd been mute. She'd been through hell herself in that basement flat, abused, whipped and beaten, bitten, scared out of her mind, but witnessing such a savage murder as a child, or even an adult, trumped that in her eyes. Had the memory of it stayed in his mind and it had broken? Had he become the Slasher? Some might say that was fanciful thinking on her part, but she'd dealt with many killers in her time, and no, it *wasn't* fanciful.

She looked into the Billy of today. He worked for Ford and Sons. Peter Ford, his father, had taken him in a week after Emma's death after a DNA test and changed his surname from Meyers to his own. Only a black Mercedes-Benz G-class SUV was registered in Billy's name, not the other vehicles that had been spotted and linked to the recent murders.

Unless he stole them...

She called down to the front desk to ask the sergeant to send plainclothes officers in an unmarked car to Billy's house, passing on what car he drove, the reg number, and for patrol to keep an eye out for it but not apprehend Billy. The rest of her team had gone home, and she needed the police there fast, so using whoever was on duty would have to do for now. She wanted him followed if he went out tonight, regardless of whether the twins had a plan to capture the Slasher. She *would* warn them, though, to be careful because officers would be in the vicinity, following him. How George and Greg proceeded after that was their lookout.

She rang Lillibet first. "I've uncovered something about Billy. His mother, a sex worker, was killed when he was eight. Going by the file, we might well be looking at him being a copycat. He witnessed her being killed, so it could have warped his brain."

"What?"

"I know, so I need you to be careful tonight, all right? If you see him, act normal—as best you can anyway. He might approach you, maybe ask you to go somewhere with him. Eyes will be on you with not only George and Greg but also the police if they follow him to where you'll be. I can't keep this under the radar here, it'll show I accessed Billy's file, and there would be questions if I didn't chase anything up. I've had to send a couple of officers in an unmarked car to Billy's and instruct them to tail him. You'll be safe so long as you don't go anywhere alone with him, do you understand?"

"Oh God. Yes, okay. Why can't you go and question him about his mum? Why do I still need to be bait?"

"Shit, you've got a point there." Janine was going to have to speak to Billy or the DCI would ask why she hadn't. *Fuck it.* "Right, I'll go there now but make out I think the person who killed his mother has started up again, not that he's a suspect."

"So you're not going to alert him to the fact you think it might be him?"

"No. The twins want to catch him."

"But you're the *police*! You should override them. It's me who has to put myself in danger. I know I said I'd do it because I want him caught, but I'm worrying now."

"I do whatever the twins want, and you should do the same. I'm sorry, but that's how it is. I'll see you soon." She ended the call and rang The Brothers. "Right, listen to me…" She explained everything before whoever had answered had a chance to speak, then waited to be bawled out if it was George. He'd give her his usual guff about answering to him and sucking it up if she didn't like it.

"It's Greg. George is in the loo. Do what you have to, I'll smooth things over with him. He won't like it that you've had to follow police protocol, but on this occasion, I can see how it'd look if you didn't query this lead. We'll still nab the Slasher, we just have to be a bit savvier about it if you've got plod after him, that's all."

"Just be careful."

"Yep."

She finished the call and contemplated going to pick Colin up to go with her, then decided against it. He wasn't much help at work anyway, and his wife had been getting on his back a lot in recent months to be home on time—and *stay* home in the evenings—so he could do without being nagged again.

She thought of Cameron. Having him driving behind her to Billy's might get him noticed and questions asked. She sent him a message not to tail her until she contacted him again. Then she nipped in to tell the DCI what she'd discovered, but he wasn't there. Frustrated, she shut her computer off then dashed downstairs and spoke to the duty sergeant, asking him if he had a spare PC she could take with her.

"Yep, Brown's available. He's catching up on his paperwork, so I'm sure he won't mind leaving it."

"Ask him to meet me in my car. Can you tell the officers who've gone to Billy's house to ignore us when we arrive, please, and to continue as planned regarding following him?"

"Yep."

She left the station and got in the driver's seat, buckling up. She had to play this carefully, couldn't fuck it up. No way did she want Billy to not go out tonight because of her visit. She'd play the concerned copper, upset on his behalf that he'd had to go through what he had, and hope he believed her.

Brown got in the passenger seat.

"I'll lead this one," Janine said. "You just sit or stand there and be quiet, okay?" On the way, she told him what the score was, leaving the twins out of it, pretending Lillibet had contacted her direct. "I want to gauge his reaction first and foremost, because it might not even be him."

"I can imagine that would have fucked him up as a kid, but copying it years later? Really?"

"Depends what the extent of the damage is in his mind and how he feels about his mother being a sex worker. That must have come as a shock. Maybe he's now taking it out on other sex workers. I can't rule it out."

"I see what you mean."

She whistled on the approach to the house, the fog shrouding it a bit. "Bloody hell. He's done well for himself. Saying that, Daddy's rich. He's Peter Ford's son."

"Ah. How the other half live, eh?"

Billy's gaff stood away from two other houses at the top of a small cul-de-sac. It must have at least six bedrooms, and because of the obvious wealth, it reminded her a bit of the house she'd been incarcerated in. She shuddered and pushed the memories aside; she had to focus on the job at hand.

The other officers had parked in someone's driveway, so they must have asked permission from the owners—that or the residents were out, which could be true as all the lights were off. Janine got out, and with Brown by her side, she knocked on Billy's door.

No one answered.

"Shit. I thought with the downstairs lights being on he'd be in." Still, she'd done this by the book, so it wasn't her fault she couldn't proceed. She rang the bell again and knocked for good measure. "Sod it, let's go."

She returned to the car. Rang the duty sergeant for an update. "Anything from the officers at Billy Ford's?"

"No sign of him, but lights are on."

"We're here now and have just discovered the same. Any news on his SUV?"

"No."

She studied the house. Maybe it was in the garage attached to the side. "Okay, then we'll be off. I'll drop Brown back and go home. Let me know if Billy or his vehicle are spotted, no matter what time it is."

"Will do."

She drove away, frustrated on one hand and relieved on the other. She'd wanted to read Billy, see if he came across as suspicious, but a bigger concern overruled her need to do that: If he wasn't indoors, where was he?

Out stalking?

Janine didn't go home. At the station, she'd searched for DI Zeller's address and arranged to go and have a chat with him. He lived in a modest terrace, a middle house with a garden readied for when spring rolled around again. Maybe he'd taken up gardening in his retirement. She knocked on the door, and an old man answered, distinguished-looking, a regal air about him. Tall, he appeared imposing. His suit trousers, and light-blue shirt collar peeking out from the V of a navy jumper, prompted her to wonder if he'd changed into those clothes because of her. They appeared too immaculate, too crisp to have been worn all day.

She held up her ID. "Thanks for seeing me."

"Come in, come in. I've missed the job so can't wait to dig in to our chat. Billy Meyers, you said. That brought back some memories, I can tell you."

He led her into an all-cream lounge, the sofas new if the taut seats and the strong scent of leather were anything to go by. A matching recliner, a half-full glass on a table beside it containing amber liquid, perhaps his favourite perch.

"Can I get you a drink?" He loitered by what must be a booze cabinet.

"Something soft for me, please."

"So you haven't clocked off for the day yet, then?"

"Unfortunately not."

"I remember it well, all that overtime." He opened the cabinet door and took a Diet Coke out. "This do you?"

"That's brilliant, thanks."

"Would you like a glass?"

"No, ta, you're all right."

He handed her the can. "Have a seat and tell me why Billy's name's cropped up after all these years. I've often thought about him. And his *father*."

Janine, picking up the stress on that word, flopped on the sofa, glad to be sitting somewhere comfy. She was tired, her bones aching. "Why say it like that?"

"Because I've always thought the father had something to do with Emma's murder, I just couldn't prove it. His alibi was rock-solid, and his bank accounts weren't suspicious—I thought he'd hired a hitman, but if he had, he hadn't paid them from any of his accounts."

"How come you went down that road?"

He told her the order of events and that Emma had kept news of Billy's existence away from Peter Ford. "Plus, the words 'Lying Bitch' were carved into her chest."

Her guts lurched. "Why isn't that in the file, then?"

He blinked several times, his dismay obvious. "It is."

"It isn't! It says there was 'wording' and a 'symbolic image' but not what was written or what that image was."

Zeller frowned. "That can't be right. I typed the report myself."

Rod fucking Clarke, got to be. That bastard had something to do with this, and I can't ask him because he's sodding well dead. "I'll check who changed it then, because that'll be logged." *But you can bet Clarke used someone else's password to make the amendments.*

Zeller nodded. "Do that, because if it's been tampered with, then there's only one conclusion we can come to."

"That someone in the force was in with the killer?"

"Or had been coerced into messing with the file. I left the job after Emma's case—the only one I never solved—and if there *had* been any tampering, I'd have thought I'd be questioned about it. I wasn't, so perhaps they caught whoever did it and I didn't need to be spoken to."

"What was your take on Rod Clarke?"

"You think it might be *him*?" Zeller laughed. "The man was a lazy bastard, did the bare minimum after he made it to DI, so I was told. He was a bit of a useless prat when I worked with him, I had to keep reminding him of what to do at scenes. It was like he only wanted his wages and the title, didn't want to do any actual work."

He could be describing Colin. "What if he *was* involved, though? I could look into his connections, see if he knew Peter before the murder. Ask Peter, even."

"But he won't tell you anything if he's the one who arranged for Emma to be killed. I'm annoyed now that I haven't been paying attention to the news. I'm aware there's this Slasher man about, but the last two weeks have been a bit hellish, and before that, I'd been dealing with my wife. She was ill, died last Wednesday. You're lucky you asked to see me today, because this is the first one in a long time where I've actually got properly dressed. Well, the first evening, because I changed out of my sloppy clothes and had a shower before you arrived. This furniture arrived today, too. The wife had a few accidents on the old one. I apologise, too much information."

"It's fine. I'm sorry for your loss."

Zeller waved it off. "She'd been poorly for months and I was expecting it. That's the one beauty, if you can call it that without sounding an arsehole, of knowing someone's going to die—it's not a shock when it happens, and in my case, I'm ashamed to say it was a relief. No more suffering for her, and no more 'when will it happen?' for me, which was agonising."

"I understand. I went through it with my mother."

"Bless you. Regina wouldn't have wanted me to go through hell while waiting for her to die, so I shouldn't berate myself too much. She'd understand why it was a relief. Anyway, enough of that. As I was saying, if I'd have been paying attention to the news like I usually would, I'd have perhaps known about the similarities—that's if they've been picked up by the papers."

"No, we've purposely kept the finer details out of the press, so you wouldn't have joined the dots anyway. But if you'd been able to call, not that I'm blaming you, I'd have known Billy might be involved sooner. Yes, I'd have checked the file and seen it had been doctored, but… You mentioned the words carved into Emma. The same applies to the four women who've been killed recently. What was the symbol on Emma's stomach?"

"A snake, serpent, whatever term you want to call it."

"That matches."

"Shit."

"Hmm. As do the breasts being stabbed at, the nipples carved with a plus sign, an X and Y on the cheeks, and the single jab to the neck, although I note in Emma's file that the knife used is different. With the recent women, the blade depth is smaller although no less deadly."

"My advice? Look into Peter Ford, see where *he's* been lately. He was my top suspect, but like I told you, I couldn't prove it was him."

Janine caught sight of the time on the mantel clock. With no word yet from the twins, Lillibet, or Debbie that they were out in the field so she could go and join them with Cameron, she reckoned she had enough time to pop and see Peter Ford. Frustrated that she had no choice, not now she'd visited Zeller and he might call in to the station and enquire how she'd got on, alerting other officers that she hadn't followed it up, she told herself that if she couldn't be there to trap the Slasher with George and Greg, tough shit. There were plenty of others to oversee things.

She thanked the ex-DI for his time, wished him well, and left, promising to let him know if Peter turned out to be their man after all. At least then Zeller could go to his grave satisfied he'd been right.

Chapter Fourteen

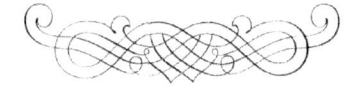

Clarke stood beside a row of wheelie bins in a bricked enclosure where they were stored for residents' use. He stared up at the nearby high-rise. Too many windows to tell if anyone watched him, but it was dark and he had a balaclava on, so it should be all right. Besides, they'd be watching the spectacle not too far away, what with several police cars parked, blue

lights flashing, and a mob of onlookers eager to watch the goings-on, not to mention jeering at the officers.

A few seconds ago, he'd peeled away from the outskirts of the large crowd that had gathered to ogle the aftermath of a shooting during a fight on a run-down housing estate. Clarke had been at the front desk in the station when the call had come in. PC Annabel Hawkins was one of the officers who'd run out to attend, and this was the perfect time to get rid of her.

This was going to be one more murder he'd tell himself he hadn't committed. He was so adept at lying that he'd even convince himself *it hadn't happened, like he'd done with Emma. There were times, when Peter brought it up, that Clarke completely forgot it had been him.*

As he'd moved away from the spectators, he'd caught Annabel's eye. He'd given her a glimpse of the gun he'd borrowed from one of his off-the-books informants who'd keep his gob shut for two hundred quid—and Clarke had promised to return it, especially as it would be sold on, and if whoever used it got caught, Annabel's murder would be pinned on them. Striations in bullets were a fucker for getting people in the shit. As the police were here searching for an active shooter, he could tell by the gleam in her eye that she wanted to be the one to apprehend him. Except he wasn't the shooter they were after, was he, but she wasn't to know that. If she brought another copper with her to find his hiding place, he'd have to shoot them an' all, but needs must.

When Zeller had left the force as soon as Emma's case had gone cold, Clarke had used Annabel's ID to log in to the system and change the file—Peter was paying him another grand to switch a few things out. But someone had noticed and questioned her about it. She'd denied doing it. Annabel had been told off for sharing her password, again she'd said she hadn't, and she was telling anyone who'd listen that she'd been framed. She shouted about it a bit too loudly for Clarke's liking, and Peter had suggested they get rid of her. As this benefited Clarke, he'd agreed.

Peter had finally given Billy permission to tell the police what had happened to his mother. The lad had described the killer—such a far cry from Peter's build that had Zeller still been on the case, he'd have to admit it wasn't Peter who'd wielded the knife, but Clarke would bet he'd still insist Peter could have paid someone else to do it.

Footsteps, one set, shoe soles crunching on the ground, brought Clarke back to the present. He waited for the second set, a colleague having Annabel's back, but nothing. He tapped the handle of the gun on the nearest bin purposely, to draw her to where he was. A torch flashed—the stupid cow was alerting him to her presence; hadn't she learned anything in training?

Another footstep, where she'd moved into the bin enclosure.

Then the bright beam picked him out.

She gasped, likely at his balaclava, and froze.

Clarke shot her in the head, glad of the silencer and the noise of the crowd. He stuffed the gun in the waistband of his trousers at the back. Ran out of the enclosure. Zipped through the streets, snatching the balaclava off halfway to his car and, once he got to it, threw himself in the driver's seat, heading for the informant's lock-up, careful to avoid street cameras. He handed the gun back then returned to the station, giving some guff that he'd popped home to see his wife who hadn't been well when he'd left home this morning. Dicky tummy to the point she'd actually shat her knickers. Maybe too much information, overegging the pudding, but it was too late now, the words were out.

And so what whether everyone tittered at his wife's fake misfortune? The job was done, and that was all he cared about.

Until the next time Peter pissed him off, wanting him to do something else.

Chapter Fifteen

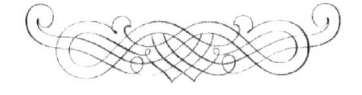

Janine nipped to the station first to check when the file had been amended. One year after the murder. The supposed officer who'd done that, a PC Annabel Hawkins, had been killed in the line of duty days later. That had Janine's scepticism alert going off. *Had* Clarke been involved? Had *he* got rid of her?

She read the file regarding Annabel's death, and, call her suspicious, but the events seemed a bit murky. No other officers around to see how she'd died when she'd been one of ten who'd been called out to attend a mass fight where a man had been shot? No civilian witnesses either when the crowd had been around sixty strong? No one who could explain why she'd gone down an alley, alone, without alerting her nearby colleagues or using her radio to send in her location, going around a corner into bin store and getting shot?

Janine would poke into this when she had more time—she wanted to scan the same date to see if Clarke had been on duty. If he hadn't, he could have somehow got wind of the shoutout to the fight and gone down there, murdered Annabel easily because everyone else must have been distracted, and if he *had* been at work, the same applied. He'd been known for sloping off on his own and giving shitty excuses as to where he'd been.

She checked the time, looked up Peter's address, and set off with Brown, arriving within ten minutes of getting behind the wheel. Ford's house, a mini mansion and set off the road at the end of a cream-coloured gravel drive, lit up in front of her headlamps, wisps of fog streaking by.

"And there I was thinking *Billy's* place was nice," she muttered. "This is another level."

"Being in finance and banking clearly pays," Brown said. "He's made a mint."

"And the rest." Janine parked and got out.

Brown joined her on the semicircular steps, three stairs up to the double-wide mahogany front doors, the panels gleaming beneath the ornate Victorian lamps either side. She couldn't press the bell because there wasn't a button. Instead, she had to tug on a silver ball attached to a chain. It sounded like Big Ben had struck.

"Blimey," Brown said.

"It probably needs to be loud because the house is so massive," Janine whispered and signalled with her eyes that they were likely being watched via a discreet camera above the door.

"Gotcha." Brown folded his hands in front of his groin. "Same deal as it would have been with the other one? Me keeping quiet?"

"Please."

One of the doors opened, and an older man stood there. Although in jeans and a polo shirt, he still appeared rich. They had that air about them, didn't they, those who were well-off. Like their clothes being of a better quality made all the difference to how they carried themselves. A brief memory of Valandra Flemington came to mind, one of the people who'd held Janine hostage. *She'd* appeared rich, too. Nice dresses, her hair in a chignon or French pleat. An aura of being wealthy about her.

She shuddered and focused on the man in front of her.

If this was Peter Ford, he'd come from a council estate upbringing yet still managed to carry off the silver-spoon effect. Maybe money helped you stand taller and peer down your nose at others, too.

I'd still be the same as I already am if I landed in a pile of cash. Snippy. A cow sometimes. All right, more than sometimes…

"Mr Ford?" she said.

He glared as if she should *know* who he was, that he'd been in the papers often enough and thought of himself as a local celebrity. She didn't give a shit *who* he thought he was, irrespective of whether he'd had anything to do with Emma's murder. If he was the Slasher, or he knew Billy was, then whatever he had in the bank and this swanky house meant jack shit. Even the rich went to prison.

"And you are?" he asked.

She held up her ID. "DI Janine Sheldon and PC Brown. Can we have a chat about your son's mother, Emma Meyers?"

His eyebrows shot up. "What for? That was *years* ago."

"I'm aware of that, I've looked into the case. There are a few things that tie it to the recent murders."

"You'd best come in, then. Do you think it's the same man?"

If it's you, yes. "Possibly."

He led them down a foyer that was larger than her living room and veered into a lounge. It was all sage-green walls and black furniture, the same green colour on some of the throw cushions, the others what might be described as oatmeal mixed with speckles of cinnamon if Janine actually gave a toss about such things. She didn't. The room, very manly, didn't have any feminine touches, unless his wife wasn't the frilly kind and was more inclined to opt for this sort of scene.

"Please take a seat. Can I get you a drink?"

Janine didn't want to bugger about waiting for him to make tea or coffee, so she declined. Peter sat, and she watched him for signs of anxiety. If he was the Slasher, he did a good job of hiding it, and if the Slasher was a copycat and Peter had only paid for Emma to be bumped off, perhaps the passing of years had helped him to stuff any nervousness away. She understood that because she'd learned to do it herself regarding her past. If you told yourself something enough, you ended up believing it: *It didn't happen. I never did that. They never did that.*

"What can I help you with?" he asked.

Janine and Brown remained standing.

Peter waved a hand towards the free sofa. "Do you not want to make yourselves comfortable?"

Brown shook his head.

Janine perched on the edge of the settee. "As I said, there are similarities that I'm concerned about. Many of the key points in Emma's murder have happened with the four victims of the current killer."

"Such as?"

"I don't need to discuss those. What I *do* need to ask is whether you had any involvement with the then DS Rod Clarke before or after Emma's murder."

Ford smiled. "That was such a shock, seeing him turn up. I went to school with him when we were little, only in primary mind you, but I remembered him well enough. I hadn't seen him since I was about eleven until he showed up with a detective regarding Emma. Zeller, I think his name was. As for when I saw him afterwards, he visited my office about one of my employees who was beaten to death."

Another murder where his name crops up?

"Why do you ask?" he queried.

"I can't divulge that as my investigation down that avenue is ongoing. Was your employee's killer ever caught?"

"Sadly, no."

"You weren't accused of anything?"

"Why would I be? I was just her boss. Clarke came to interview my staff."

I'll nose into that. "I have to ask this, and please don't be angry, but where were you on…" She pulled the last four murder dates out of her mind and repeated them to him.

Peter shook his head as if she amused him. "You think it's me? That I killed Emma, then years later decided to do it again? I took early retirement and have been far too busy to even contemplate doing anything other than going on holiday, playing golf, and eating long lunches with my wife and occasionally my sons."

"You didn't answer me. Where were you?"

He took a phone out of his pocket and consulted it, perhaps an online calendar. "The first one, I was in Dubai. The second, on a cruise ship in the Med. The third, in Jersey—we went straight from the cruise to there. Stayed with one of our clients I happened to become friends with during the course of business."

"Do you have evidence of that?"

He rattled off the friend's name, number, and address, Brown writing them down, then got up and went to a sideboard. He found a beige file and handed it to her. On the front, a label: Holidays.

"Everything you need is in there. If you want copies, I can scan them for you. And if you'd like to see my photos that go with all three trips, complete with timestamps—hell, even take my phone with them on to get proof of when and where they were taken—be my guest."

Janine flicked through the papers. "This is fine for now, but if my boss wants copies, I'll get back to you." She placed the file beside her. "Where is your wife?"

"Ah, she's on holiday number four, off in Jamaica with her niece. Bloody daft of her if you ask me, it's hurricane season what with it being November, but there's no telling her. If you need to speak to her, I can give you her number."

"I don't think we will, but we'll take it anyway."

He looked at Brown and recited it. "So, now that we've established that I can't possibly be the Slasher, was there anything else?"

Janine leaned forward a bit. "You didn't mention where you were last night."

"At a charity gala. Again, you can check that. Contact Kara Weststaff at the Bellson Institute. I suspect it'll be covered in the local news."

Here was where Janine shifted things and got Peter onside so he didn't think she was getting close to revealing the killer's identity. "Can I just ask, how did Billy handle what he witnessed when Emma was killed?"

"God, are you going to blame *him* now?" He chuckled, so sure of himself it was sickening.

"No, not at all. I was thinking more about the children who've been left behind with the other four women's murders. Do you have any pointers I can pass on?" She prepared her lie. "One of them has selective mutism—choosing to speak of anything but how he's feeling regarding his mother's death. I noted in the file that Billy was completely mute for a while, then moved to selective. I hope it's okay for me to ask this of you. I wouldn't want to offend…"

"Of course you haven't offended me. If I can help those other children, then I don't mind. Billy was so traumatised that at first he never spoke at all, as you've mentioned—I have to say, it was frustrating for myself and the police, but speaking from my point of view, I was desperate for him to say something about it as I was a suspect. No matter that I had an alibi that checked out, et cetera. When he *did* eventually speak, he wouldn't mention that night, how he felt about it, nothing, so I paid for him to see a therapist. *She* couldn't get anything out of him for ages either, then one day, a year or so after it had happened, he came to me after a session with her and it all spilled out. Whatever she'd said to him must have unlocked his memories. Of course, I phoned the police right away, encouraged him to tell them, too, and as far as I could see, it was clear that the man who'd gone to Emma's house every night for weeks was the man who'd killed her."

"I saw the description of him wasn't any help because the witness said it was dark out so she couldn't really see."

"Hmm, so that didn't help me either when it came to clearing my name, but Billy remembered. The man's build wasn't the same as mine, but Zeller still kept on, trying to pin it on me. I ended up believing he was one of those officers who, when he had an idea in mind, wouldn't let go of it no matter what the evidence said. I was glad when he went into retirement as I was left alone, then. I did *not* kill Emma, I can swear on that, nor did I hire a hitman. I wouldn't know where to start in looking for an assassin, for goodness sake."

But what about a friend? "So, getting back to what we were talking about: you suggest the children go to therapy."

"Yes."

Janine stood. "Okay, thank you for your time, and sorry to disturb your evening."

Peter rose. "Absolutely not a problem."

"Oh," she said, halfway out of the lounge doorway. "How is Billy now?"

"He's fine."

"He works for your company, yes?"

"On paper." He smirked.

"What does that mean?"

"He has what I call a hobby in one of his garages."

"Which is?"

"Repairing vehicles."

"Where's his garage? I might give him a bell to get mine serviced."

"At the back of his house. He's a trained mechanic. He does number plates as well, valeting, all that kind of thing. Pin money, and it keeps him out of mischief."

I don't think it bloody does. Janine's stomach rolled over. *The cars used in the murders. Fucking hell, what if they're ones he was asked to fix and he used them with false plates? He valets so could have got the blood off.*

"That must be nice for him," she said. "And I'm glad he's okay. Thanks again."

She headed into the hall, Brown beside her. Peter saw them out, and Janine drove away, her heart missing beats.

"What's up?" Brown asked.

Janine told him.

"Fucking hell," Brown said. "That sounds suss. Will you apply for a warrant to search his garage?"

"On what grounds?" She put her foot down, going towards the station. "I could be putting two and two together and coming up with the wrong sodding answer here."

"But what if you're not?"

Janine sighed. What the fuck should she do? "I'll drop you off then contact the DCI. He can make the call on that one." By the time he made a decision, the Slasher might already have been caught by the twins.

She glanced at the clock on the dash. Coming up to eight o'clock. Why the hell hadn't her burner tinkled to let her know Lillibet and Debbie had gone out?

I need to calm down.

She drove on, remembering she hadn't let Cameron know she was okay and that he could follow her again now

Something else for her to worry about, him fretting over her.

183

Chapter Sixteen

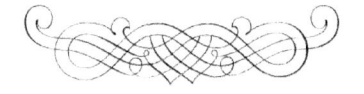

Lillibet and Debbie sat at the bar in The Angel. Everyone was in place, and while Lillibet felt safe that she was being protected, she still couldn't get over how a car had followed their taxi from her house to here. It *had* to be the Slasher, but Debbie, who'd turned round regularly to check through the rear window on the way, hadn't been able to see the driver through the fog which had got thicker since they'd been getting glammed up—plus the car had stayed well back. It had stopped near the pub, so it had tailed them, but Debbie had ushered Lillibet inside before she'd had a chance to see if the driver had got out.

Maxwell and Nate had stayed behind with their dog in case the Slasher went there at any point to wait for Lillibet to return. At the minute, though, Billy sat close by, and she couldn't get past the feeling of his eyes boring into the back of her head.

She smiled to pretend she wasn't afraid, and Debbie nattered on about how Moon had just sent her a message saying he'd been roped into smoking weed in Amsterdam tonight and he felt a bit sick.

Lillibet could do with a joint right about now, to calm her, make her think everything would be okay. She had a sinking feeling in the pit of her stomach that told her it wouldn't, though.

But she *had* to trust the twins. They were good at what they did, well used to dealing with people like Billy or the Slasher. Debbie had said there were times when things had gone tits up, but in the end, The Brothers had won whatever battle they'd stormed into.

But what if this time they don't?
What if Billy is *the Slasher and he kills me?*

Chapter Seventeen

Ichabod, his fake beard and glasses in the glove box now, watched their target in The Angel who sat in the far corner to the left of the front doors, where people usually played darts or wasted coins on the fruit machine. Billy — or Slasher if Ichabod's instincts were correct — hadn't done anything to warrant being asked to step outside for a wee chat. Yet. Billy presented himself as normal customer material, apart from staring a bit too often at Lillibet and Debbie, who hadn't seemed to notice he was there. That would all be for show, though. Going by the messages Ichabod had received from the twins during the course of his surveillance, if Billy approached Lillibet, she had to act surprised to see him. Pleased, even.

On his travels following him here, despite the fog, Ichabod thought Billy had seen him in his rearview mirror more than once, so either Ichabod was getting crap at this side hustle craic or Billy was extra-vigilant because of what he planned to do—what he'd possibly *been* doing to those dead women. If he *wasn't* the Slasher—*I swear tae God, I'll eat my feckin' hat if he isn't, so I will*—then he was at the very least a stalker pervert, obsessed with Lillibet.

A bit like Katy Marlborough is with me.

Ichabod could have screamed at the sight of that very woman coming towards him now. She'd been a pain in his arse at Jackpot Palace for weeks, approaching him if she saw him working there. He usually spotted her before she spotted him, and he went off to do things off the casino floor while she was in attendance, but every now and then she snuck in without him noticing, creeping up behind him and shouting, "Surprise!" Not difficult to do. The casino was three shop units wide, so if he was at the other end with his back to the other sections, he had no chance of escape.

Seemed he didn't have an escape this evening either. She stood in front of him and smiled, blocking his view of Billy. Ichabod moved to the side a little so his sight was clear, wishing he could tell this woman to feck off.

"Fancy seeing you here," Katy said. "Very rare that you're not at work. I've just been there, and they said you'd taken the evening off. You told me you don't socialise much."

"I don't…"

"Yet here you are."

Annoyance prodded him. Who did she think she was, questioning him? "I *am* allowed tae go out without havin' tae explain myself tae ye, ye know."

"Ooh, touchy. Has someone annoyed you today?"

"Tae be honest, *ye're* annoyin' me. I don't want tae offend ye, but if ye don't back off, I will."

"Offend me how? Go on, try it, see if it works."

It was as if she didn't pick up on social cues—or she didn't care *who* she pissed off as long as she got her way. And what she wanted—and had been clear about from the start—was to date Ichabod. He didn't fancy her, he was still hung up on a classy woman he couldn't have, the beautiful Marleigh Jasper, who was happily married, so she'd said, and besides, Katy wasn't his type. Too brash. Too forward.

Ichabod flicked his attention from Billy to Katy and stared her in the eye. "I don't want tae go out with ye. I'm not attracted tae ye. Leave me alone."

Her face clouded for the beat of one second, then her expression brightened, and she spat out her annoying, trilly-arsed laugh. "Oh, don't be daft. You're playing hard to get, that's all."

He *had* to get rid of her. "I'm tellin' ye, I don't want anythin' tae do wid ye. Walk away and don't ask me tae got out wid ye again. It's borderin' on harassment. If this were the other way round, me badgerin' ye, I'd be carted down the nick for bein' a sex pest."

She blinked in shock, obviously used to men fawning over her; that Ichabod wasn't had seemed to touch a raw nerve. "How rude."

"I've had tae be, because ye won't take no for an answer."

She opened her mouth to say more, but a big hand landed on her left shoulder.

George, in a ginger wig and beard, growled in a Scottish accent, "Fuck off."

Jimmy Riddle, roped in to help with capturing the Slasher, appeared at her right side, slapping his hand on her other shoulder. "And don't bother the customers again."

They escorted her away. Ichabod sagged with relief, although the incident had drawn eyes in his direction, including Billy's. Ichabod raised the glass of lemonade he hoped passed as a vodka and tonic, effectively telling everyone to mind their own business.

Billy switched his attention to Lillibet, so for now, all was well.

Chapter Eighteen

Although plenty of the twins' people stood around Lillibet acting as customers, her nerves still fizzled now Debbie had nipped to the toilet. There was something comforting about having that woman beside her. Debbie was a tower of strength just by being there and probably didn't even realise it.

Lillibet sipped her lemonade, although to anyone watching, it looked like she had vodka in it. Debbie had arranged for an empty bottle to be filled with water and should only be used for those who needed to pretend to drink alcohol. Lisa, the pub manager, was the only one who could serve the people who were in on this charade of an evening, the rest of the staff warned to keep away from the players.

Earlier in the day, Lillibet had felt better about the Slasher being Billy, because at least she could try to talk him round if he *did* get her alone, but once Janine had phoned to confirm she *really* thought it could be him, things had changed. Lillibet's feelings on being bait had veered out of control on that call, and panic had sent her dizzy. Debbie had calmed her down afterwards, reminding her that The Brothers had brought in their best people to deal with this, and Moon's men, Alien and Brickhouse, who were running the Moon estate between them while their boss was in Amsterdam, had also come over to 'blend in' with the customers in The Angel, although blend in they did not. Especially with George and Greg here in disguise, too, all four of them big and easily noticeable.

She'd sensed Billy's eyes on her all night so far, his reflection creeping her out in the mirror behind the bar. She felt ransacked, violated by his constant perusal of her, and it bothered her what might be going through his mind. Did he hate her and that's why she was next on his list? Or did he *like* her and that was why?

God, it might not even be him.

He sat wedged between the wall and a fruit machine, likely thinking that spot shielded him from the majority's view, or maybe it gave him the illusion of being safe and protected like Debbie did for her. What had happened to him as a child may mean he suffered from anxiety if exposed too much. Now she knew he'd witnessed his mother being killed, she had sympathy for him, but that didn't mean he had an excuse to go around killing women, did it. How bad must it have been to warp his brain like that? How could he think it was right to put another woman through what his mum had endured?

Debbie came back, and the evening moved on, Billy only getting up once more to buy another drink, acting as if he didn't know they were there. A short time later, Lillibet relaxed when he stood and left the pub, a black puffa jacket hanging over one arm—the same sort of jacket Balaclava Man had on when he'd posted that note through her letterbox.

Oh God.

Either he'd got bored waiting for her to leave, he'd gone off to wait outside for her, or he wasn't the Slasher—loads of people had a coat like that.

Ichabod went to follow him, but the woman who'd been steered away by George and Jimmy earlier sailed into his path, placing a hand on his chest. Face like thunder, Ichabod sidestepped, but the woman mimicked his movement.

Lillibet shifted her attention to Jimmy Riddle, also trying to push his way past customers intent on standing in his way—The Angel was bloody packed. Sonny Bates stood from his bar stool. Ginger George, who'd been parked by the doors to the toilets for most of the night, carved a channel through the crowd, and Greg, his shoulder-length blond wig swinging beneath a red baseball cap, wisps of hair catching on a scraggly ZZ Top beard, rushed from the corner opposite where Billy had been sitting and headed for the door. Alien and Brickhouse shot up from their booth seat beneath the big clock on the wall at the end nearest the toilets. It all happened so quickly yet not quickly enough, and by the time all the men bar Ichabod had gone outside, Lillibet had a nasty feeling Billy would be long gone by now.

Debbie stared at her. "Fuck. *That* didn't go very well, did it."

Lillibet shivered. "No."

"There's too many customers for it to have worked. George will be fuming. He doesn't like it when things go tits up."

Funny, that, neither do I, seeing as it's me who could be killed.

Lillibet didn't like the sensation of drowning that took over her, and she battled through it, clutching the edge of the bar.

"It'll be all right," Debbie said. "You'll see."

But what if it isn't?

Chapter Nineteen

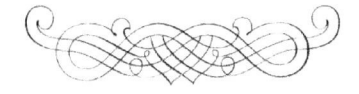

Slasher had got lucky. When he'd left the pub, a crowd of smokers had hidden him from view, as had the thicker fog and the long, snaking queue of people from The Roxy, which had enabled him to sidle past them all and leg it down the side of the pub. A security light had splashed on, so he'd dived round the back. He'd shrugged his coat on and hoisted himself over the wrought-iron fence, the tops of two pole points digging into his belly. He'd run towards the graveyard, staggering between headstones and weird monuments that had loomed out of the fog. Lillibet had been watched by people all evening, he was sure of it, and once he'd fully convinced himself of that fact, he'd bolted. He'd also convinced himself they knew he was after her, which was why he hadn't got in his car— someone would likely be stationed outside in the eventuality he walked out. Were the watching people the police?

In the middle of the cemetery, he panted beside a statue of Jesus who clasped his hands over the grave in front of him, head bent as though he was upset the person in the coffin was dead. Person. That's what Billy referred to *her* as in his darkest moments, not Mum, not the woman he'd *thought* she'd been before everything had gone wrong. That was all a lie according to Dad, a façade she'd erected so Billy thought she was the best thing since sliced bread. Sometimes, though, he inspected his memories and couldn't see *how* she'd have faked laughing with him on those days they'd spent time together, or when he'd caught her in an unguarded moment, a small smile on her lips where she'd watched him playing with Mr Spencer. She *had* loved him, no matter how much Dad tried to say she hadn't, and now, the clarity of that walloped him in the gut as it tended to do from time to time.

Going out to sell herself to put food in his belly.

Letting men paw her so she could keep the electric on and her son warm.

Saving up to take him on holiday to Southend.

Taking him to town and buying him new shoes and clothes, even using up her last few quid to get Mr Spencer for him off that market stall.

If she didn't love him, she wouldn't have done all that, would she?

His mind switching back and forth between what he truly believed and what Dad *wanted* him to believe had always been difficult. Confusing. Terrifying—especially when he came out of his 'I love her' phase and was dumped violently back into hating her. Now, this second, he could see it all so clearly, how Dad had manipulated him, planted his words inside his head, steered the way he had to go, to think, to feel.

"I'm sorry, Mum," he whispered. He went down on his knees, the damp of the grass seeping through his trousers. "But he won't let up. He just keeps on and on about you. I'm not allowed to love you, not anymore. Not if I want to keep the house and have the money. He'll take it all off me if I don't do what he wants."

Mum's influence had only lasted eight short years, whereas Dad's was so much longer than that, enough to erase most of what Mum had taught Billy—how to be kind, to see things from the other side, to have compassion, sympathy, and empathy. Maybe, as he'd thought once before, his hatred for her wasn't because Dad had planted those seeds but because she'd put herself in the position to get killed by that punter. If she wasn't going out there, selling herself, she'd never have met him.

Dad was convinced it was the shadow man who'd come that night so long ago to kill her, the one saying he'd given Mum an extra fifty quid by accident. Billy had to keep it quiet that Dad had sent him away after punching him, that he'd visited each night, and to tell the police Shadow Man had been the one to speak through the letterbox. Otherwise, if they knew it was Dad, they'd say *he'd* killed her, *then* who would Billy have lived with? Mum's family hadn't wanted him, and Dad had insisted Michaela wouldn't be allowed to adopt him. Billy would have been taken back into care, and he'd hated the week he'd spent with that foster family.

So many children squashed into one house, their ages ranging from a newborn to this bitch of a bully girl who'd made his life hell. Fourteen, she was, but looking back on it, knowing what her words had meant now he had an adult's perspective, she'd had the knowledge of someone so much older than that.

"Can't speak or won't speak?" Nicola walked into the bedroom he shared with another boy, Henry, and closed the door, leaning on it. "You're a fucking freak, d'you know that?" Arms folded, she smirked. "I heard about what happened to you. They need to learn to keep their voices down around here." She sniffed. "Tell me what you saw when your mum copped it."

Billy didn't want to, he couldn't risk Mr Black coming to find him, so he shook his head. She glared at him, her stare so hard he flinched. He gripped Mr Spencer tighter.

"Did he stick his cock in her? Did you like seeing that? Did he put it in her mouth?"

Billy's eyes prickled.

"I bet he did. Did he put his hands all over her tits?" She shoved off the door and stalked closer, bending so her face loomed over his. *"Did you get hard?"*

He didn't know what she meant and shook his head.

"Maybe you didn't because you're a kid, I dunno, but I bet if you were a man and you'd seen all that, you'd have come in your pants." Her Wotsit-scented breath landed on his face, the corners of her mouth tinted orange from the crisps.

Her words, they didn't mean anything to him. Why was she saying them if they didn't make sense?

"She was a slag, so Alice and Kyle said."

Alice and Kyle, the mum and dad who looked after them. Alice was nice, she cuddled Billy, and if he closed his eyes, he almost thought it was Mummy. Kyle was all right, too, although he told them off if they got too loud, and he didn't like elbows on the table when they were eating dinner, he said it was rude.

Billy wanted to ask Nicola what a slag was but didn't. Sometimes it was so hard not speaking, so he bit his tongue a lot to stop himself from opening his mouth.

"Men paid her for sex, did you know that? So those clothes they let you bring with you, they were bought with dirty money. Pervert money. My mum was like yours, except she let men do it with me an' all, which

is why I'm here. It hurts when they shove their dick in, just so you know. In case you get put with someone else soon and they do it to you."

Billy didn't know where he was going next, no one had told him, but he reckoned, if the test said Peter was his dad, he could go to his big house and swim in the pool. People had come the other day, a woman and a policeman, and had put one of those long cotton buds in his mouth.

Nicola scowled. "I bet you get lucky and your old man will take you. It's all right for some." She drew her head away from him and returned to the door. "I hate you for that."

She sloped out, and he stared at the landing where Henry played with his trucks on the floor. Henry looked up at Billy and waved him over, but Billy continued to hold Mr Spencer.

He didn't need anyone else if he had his soldier.

"I'll never forgive you for putting me in that position, Mum."

Slasher stood, his trousers sticking to his knees for a moment then peeling away, and the movement of that fabric, the parting of it from his skin, was a reminder of how he and his mother were no longer connected. It stung, that she'd engineered her own death by taking the path she had. Why hadn't she loved him enough to stay home at night and be a shop assistant while he was at school?

"The conviction. Even then, your choices sent you to where you ended up."

The thud of sprinting footsteps had him spinning to check his surroundings.

"Keep looking," someone shouted. "I heard voices. Maybe he's got an accomplice. Shit!"

Slasher stared into the fog, seeing no one. He got his thoughts in order, his head on straight. Whoever had been watching in The Angel had come to find him, they'd seen him leaving. They wouldn't expect him to head *back* there but away from it, so he quickly and quietly set off, working out what he should do when he'd climbed over the fence. If he stood in the corner of the pub car park, someone getting into their vehicle would soon see him once their headlamps or the security light clicked on. But if he stood down by the fire exit door at the back, to the side of it, so when it opened outwards he'd be shielded from view, he could wait it out until The Roxy had closed and everyone had gone home, then make a dash for it to his car out the front. Yes, he'd likely be followed by someone already waiting for him in *their* car, but he could lose them in the streets if he drove fast enough.

Police, it had to be the police. But *why* had he been watched? What had he done to alert them to the fact he was the Slasher? Nothing as far as he could recall. Unless Lillibet had been asked if anyone had bothered her lately, been weird, and she'd told them about talking to him earlier in The Angel, then him ringing her this afternoon. She hadn't seen him in quite some time until today, so maybe it *had* looked weird and it seemed like he'd suddenly popped up out of nowhere, bothering her for a date. Were the police that desperate to find the killer they'd latched on to that scenario and run with it?

Mr Spencer whispered that his father had killed Mum, and the voice wouldn't go away. What if it was? No, Mr Black had been too skinny. But what if Dad had paid someone to do it like that detective had thought?

Back over the fence, he situated himself beside the fire exit and leaned on the rear wall of the pub. Drew his hood up. Took is balled-up gloves from one of the pockets and slid them on. It was getting colder, and he'd likely freeze if he stood still for too long, but it wasn't like he could jog on the spot to generate warmth, was it? A security guard stood on the other side of that door and would hear him.

A lock mechanism clicked, and he jumped, holding his breath, expecting the fire door to open. But a shaft of light cut into the fog a couple of metres along, and a woman stepped out of another doorway in what he assumed was a dressing gown, triggering the security lamp. The illumination stretched to her, almost reached him, so he silently moved along a bit, into the darkness beyond the beam's outer edge. The door closed behind her, and she lit up a cigarette, the fog shrouding her enough that she appeared as a ghost inside misty whiteness.

He thought of the ghosts in his childhood home and pushed one hand into his pocket. Wrapped his fingers around Mr Spencer.

He'd be okay now.

And so would she.

Chapter Twenty

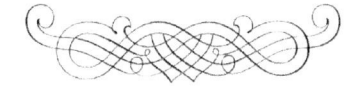

George left the cemetery via the gap between the front gates and a hedge. He met up with Greg, Alien, Brickhouse, and Jimmy. The fucking bastard fog had hampered their search, seeming denser back there, what with it being open space. For all they knew, Billy could still be in amongst the gravestones and monuments, laughing his arse off that he'd got away. No word had come from Will, who sat outside The Angel in a car, to let them know Billy had reappeared there, but his earlier message explaining why he hadn't seen him leaving hadn't been needed. George had seen it well enough for himself. He'd battled through a crowd of smokers and noted the end of the queue for The Roxy had reached the pub.

Of all the fucking luck that bastard has.

Will had said Billy hadn't got in his car, he was sure of that.

George had questioned those in the queue closest to the pub, and someone had mentioned the security light coming on and a man running past the parked cars. George had shouted to the others where he thought Billy had gone—all done in his Scottish accent—and told them the plan: George, Greg, and Alien checking down the back of the pub then vaulting the fence; Jimmy and Brickhouse pelting it round the corner to the cemetery entrance; and Ichabod, who'd come out later than them because of that bloody Katy woman, remaining outside The Angel in case Billy came back.

Despite all that, the fog—and Billy—had won.

"He could be anywhere by now," the Canadian Alien muttered.

George sighed. Checked his phone. "No one's messaged, so he hasn't gone back to the pub. You and Brickhouse may as well call it a night. Cheers for your help, though."

Alien nodded, then he and his sidekick blended into the fog. It gave George the creeps that it had swallowed them up so easily and quickly, and his mind went into overdrive, whispering that Billy could be standing mere feet away and they wouldn't know. How had it thickened so fast in the time they'd been standing here?

"It's a fucking bust," Greg said.

"What do you want me to do now?" Jimmy asked.

"Go home or whatever you want," George said. He lowered his voice in case Billy loitered. "Me and Greg will concentrate our efforts on The Angel. He'll have to come back for his car at some point. Janine's got coppers outside his house, so he's fucked if he goes back there, although because he hasn't done anything and there's no proof, all Janine can do is question him about his mother's murder—if he even goes home. I got a text from her earlier when we were in the pub, and she's had to go and see his father. Maybe that was why Billy got up and walked out. His dad could have messaged, told him Janine had come sniffing. He could have picked him up and taken him to *his* house."

"What," Greg said quietly, "so you reckon his dad knows he's the Slasher?"

"Who can tell? Some people have odd relationships with their kids. Maybe he sent his son out to kill women as revenge."

"Then you two go to his father's," Jimmy suggested. "I'll go back and stand near Lillibet and Debbie at the bar, just in case."

George nodded. "That's not a bad shout, actually. You've got our other men in The Angel anyway if you need a hand. Assuming Billy goes back inside."

Happier now they had a new plan in place, George walked back round with them, the fog clearer in patches but more concentrated in others. Jimmy went into the pub. In the BMW down the side, George gunned the engine, waiting for Greg who'd gone to the corner of the building to peer down the back in the light of the security lamp.

Greg got in the car. "It's too thick to see fuck all."

"No matter what Janine's said, it might not even be him we're after. He could have just left and decided not to drive because of the weather."

"Odd that he didn't go up to Lillibet, though. Even when he bought a drink, he didn't look her way, yet he knew she was there because he stared at her for most of the night."

"Maybe because Debbie told him to fuck off on the phone this afternoon he thought better of speaking to Lillibet. You know what Deb can be like when she gets arsey."

Greg chuckled. "Yep."

"What I don't like is not knowing for sure that Billy's our man. We could be fucking about with him, thinking he's the Slasher, when all he's guilty of is fancying Lillibet and wanting to take her on a date. All the while, the real Slasher's out there, stalking his next woman."

"Come on, enough speculating. Get hold of Janine for the dad's address. She's going to want to know why she wasn't called out to be in on this tonight."

"Yeah, well, I decided she wasn't needed."

George phoned her, got the information, and cut the call when she asked what he wanted it for. That would piss her off, but he didn't give a shit.

He reversed out of the car park, The Roxy queue gone now, and drove away.

He chuckled. "Turning up in these disguises… He's going to wonder who the fuck is on his doorstep."

"Not to mention being naffed off because we're dropping round so late. Not that I give a toss."

"Me neither."

Chapter Twenty-One

Peter, still unnerved by the visit from the police, thought through everything that had been discussed. Had he come across as too confident? That was his go-to demeanour when he'd run the business, giving investors and whatnot the impression he knew his stuff and they could trust him. It had worked—he'd become well-known for his business acumen and donating to local charities, making it into the papers time and again. The fact the woman officer hadn't seemed to know who he was had annoyed him, but he supposed he couldn't expect *everyone* to realise his good standing in the community.

Thank goodness Michaela was out of the way. She'd have had another mini stroke if she'd been here, listening to the past being dragged up again. The stress she'd been under while helping to bring Billy up had finally taken its toll—he'd been a difficult bugger to say the least, such a moody child and an even moodier adult. Six months ago, when he'd done something or other to add to his long list of stupid behaviours, Michaela had suffered a transient ischaemic attack.

I should have cut him out of our lives then. Got rid of the bad egg.

The holidays Peter and Michaela had indulged in had been for relaxation, recuperation, to take her mind away from the son she'd so readily welcomed into her arms but who'd cruelly rejected her as his second mother. Yes, Peter had ensured Billy hated Emma, but his firstborn had never come round to the idea of Michaela replacing her, as if he felt *all* mothers were bad. Michaela had never tried to jump into Emma's spot as if the woman had never existed, but she'd wanted some kind of acknowledgement that she'd been there for him through thick and thin. She was a worrier, and Billy's antics had ramped up her anxiety. Her getting poorly had been the wake-up call Peter had needed.

It had been clear since Emma's murder that Billy wasn't all there up top—had it twisted his mind? *Of course it bloody did.* They'd put it down to trauma, as had his therapist, but his obsession with that toy soldier and his tendency to go inside his head had been a worrying concern—and an irritation to Peter. He'd wanted two sons, and he'd got them, but Billy was a far cry from Darren who'd strolled into the business as though born to it and never gave them a moment's trouble.

Billy takes after Emma. Shit follows him wherever he goes.

Billy always had an issue. Billy always needed attention. Billy, Billy, Billy…

Peter jumped at the sound of the doorbell ringing. Had the police come back? Had they found new evidence after all these years and their visit earlier had been to test the waters? With

Clarke and that PC woman dead, plus the lead DI retiring, he'd thought it was over, he was free, but that may not be the case.

Peter recalled what DI Sheldon had said. *Many of the key points in Emma's murder have happened with the four victims of the current killer...* What did that mean? The newspapers hadn't revealed much, just that the prossers had been "butchered", but didn't journalists always big things up to sell papers? But what if a copycat was out there, someone who'd known exactly what had happened to Emma's body? Was it a member of the police force? A civilian who worked at the station with access to the files? A person Clarke had confided in?

Or someone who'd watched it all unfold?

Billy? Shit!

What if Zeller had crawled out of the woodwork to point out those key points, leading Sheldon to Peter's door? Clarke had removed the specifics from the file, so any searches Sheldon would have done wouldn't have thrown up Emma's case, but what if it had been flagged anyway with some obscure word she'd plugged into the database? It must have done, otherwise, why would she have come here?

Fucking hell.

With no time to contact his son to question him as to what he'd been up to, if he even had, Peter straightened his shirt collar and went to answer the door. He peered through the peephole. Two men stood on the top step, one blond with a baseball cap and long beard, the other red-haired with a shorter beard. The ginger fella had black thick-framed glasses over assessing eyes. Bloody hell, they looked like they were members of that pikey family who'd camped out a mile or so away. The sods had cluttered the field up with their caravans and rubbish, and the locals were up in arms.

He reminded himself he wasn't supposed to think of them that way, pikey was an offensive word these days. What were they now? Travellers? They were probably after some metal scraps or whatever it was they dealt in, although why they thought he'd have any was a mystery, and at this time of night? It could have waited until the morning.

He swung the door wide.

"Can I help you?" He kept the door open enough that he could see but closed enough that he could shut it quickly if they turned nasty. They were big men and quite intimidating now he came to think about it, and last week, one of the travellers had punched the farmer who owned the field they'd commandeered.

"Where's Billy?" Ginger asked, his accent Scottish.

Billy? He hadn't lived there for years, so why come here? They'd packed him off to his own house once it became clear he enjoyed winding Michaela up. Peter gave him money as if he worked at the office; he hadn't wanted him there unless he had to be present for meetings. Peter funded his lifestyle, and Billy had his little garage business. Peter had thought that had kept him occupied, but maybe it hadn't been enough.

"I have no idea…" he said. "Why do you need to speak to him?" *Why am I asking? I promised Michaela I'd take a step back.*

"We've come to collect," the Scottish one said.

"He owes us money." This from the blond, an Irish brogue that sounded distinctly off. "Borrowed it from us, so he did, and we want it back."

"I don't know anything about that." *What's their game? Have they seen I've got a bob or two and came to chance their arm?* "Are we done here?"

"If ye could tell us where he is," Blond said, "that would be grand."

"If you don't," Ginger butted in, "then we'll hurt you."

Peter swallowed. He didn't doubt that statement. These bruisers wouldn't think twice about thumping him.

Play their game. "Let me give him and ring and ask him where he is, all right? Then you can go direct to him, as this is all news to me. He doesn't live here, you see. Hasn't for a long time."

"We know where he lives, and he isn't there." Blond pointed to the top step. "Come out here and do it so we can see if ye're up tae any funny business."

"Well, that's a bit…a bit much. I don't feel comfortable going outside. I don't know you."

"Ye will if ye don't do as ye're told. Ye'll know us more than ye would've liked."

Peter went to close the door on them, scared now.

"Don't bother." Ginger produced a gun from God knew where.

Peter's heart felt as if it might burst from fear. "Oh, come on, there's no need for that, is there?"

"Seems there is, because ye won't do as ye're told," Blond said. "Outside, now, or he shoots yer little piggies off."

As if they didn't want to be hurt, Peter's feet moved before his brain had engaged, and he found himself on the step, although he was somewhat reassured that his door was still open and the safety of his house was behind him. Not to mention the security camera above the lintel.

He glanced up at it.

Ginger smiled. "This is just a friendly chat, but switch that off."

Friendly? In what scenario is a gun friendly?

Peter swallowed again. "I'll have to g-go inside to d-do that. The panel, it's j-just there."

"On you go, then."

Peter walked indoors, and under the watchful eye of Ginger who'd followed him, he disabled the camera feed.

"Move," Ginger said.

Peter leapt out of the way, contemplating running upstairs to lock himself in one of the bathrooms. No, he'd be chased. Caught. Shot.

Ginger used the butt of the gun and bashed the feed display unit, glass tinkling on the floor.

"Was there really any need for that?" Peter blurted, annoyed he'd defaced his property.

Ginger wrenched the white plastic casing off the wall and yanked at the wires. He put the gun in his waistband and took a knife out of his pocket, cutting them. "Does this record?"

"No."

"Are you *sure*?"

"Y-yes!"

"If I find out otherwise, I'll use this to slice your fucking throat." Ginger brandished the knife and waved it about.

"I swear to you, it's just a d-door camera, it shows me who's t-there, and that's all."

"Back outside." Ginger chivvied Peter onto the step. "Ring Billy."

Unsure whether any move to take his phone from his pocket would be misconstrued, he said, "I need to g-get my m-mobile."

"Do it, then!" Ginger barked. "Fuck me, you're a bugging wee bastard."

"Okay, okay!" Peter pulled his phone out and prodded in the unlock code.

"Show us the screen so we can see if ye're ringin' the right person," Blond said. "I mean, ye finger could slip and ye end up dialin' nine-nine-

nine, which would piss us off." He glared. "And ye don't want tae do that."

No, I don't.

Peter held the phone up, his hand shaking, and selected Billy's name from his contact list. He visually checked in with them that he could press it, and at their nods, he poked the screen.

"Put it on speaker," Ginger ordered, slipping the knife away and grabbing the gun again.

Peter obeyed. He just wanted these men away from here.

Maybe we should relocate. Michaela would feel better if we lived in the countryside.

Ringing trilled then stopped.

"Dad? What do you want?" Billy whispered.

Peter frowned. "Why the *hell* are you whispering?"

"I've got people after me and I'm hiding."

"I know, they're standing in front of me."

"Shit. The police?"

"No, two men. You seem to owe them money."

"*What*?"

Peter sighed. "How much do you want this time, Billy? Have you got a gambling problem or something now? Drugs? Something else that will upset Michaela?"

"No!"

"Then why have you borrowed money instead of asking me?"

"I haven't."

An unpleasant hot swirl set up home in Peter's stomach. Billy was lying again. *I'm so sick of it*. "They say you have."

"I haven't. Listen, I need to talk to you about something. Can they hear me?"

Ginger shook his head and raised the gun.

"No," Peter said, his arsehole spasming. What the devil was going on? If Billy didn't owe them, what did they want? "What do you need to tell me?"

"I've done something," Billy whispered. "And I need your help before I do it again."

"*What* have you done?"

A long pause. Ginger raised his eyebrows as if to chivvy Peter into pushing Billy for an answer.

"Billy?" Peter prompted. "Are you still there?"

"I killed those women." Billy had said it fast, like he always did when he admitted to something he'd done wrong. As if by saying it quickly he couldn't change his mind.

Ginger put the gun to Peter's temple, his expression so dark it frightened Peter more than his son telling him he was the Slasher. That was what he was saying, wasn't it?

"What women?" Peter asked to get confirmation.

"Those fucking bitches like Mum. I did what *you* did and got rid of them."

Peter scrunched his eyebrows for the men's benefit. But fuck, had Billy worked out he'd got Clarke to kill Emma? How?

Fuck getting done for this. "You did what *I* did? I don't have the faintest idea what you're talking about."

"You killed my mum, didn't you?"

Peter snorted. "I most certainly did not! Where did you get *that* idea from?"

"It *had* to be you. Even that policeman thought it was."

"Billy, I had an alibi, you *know* that. It was Shadow Man." At a weird look from Blond, Peter felt he had to elaborate so they understood. "That man who kept coming to the door, remember? *He* did it. I know I disliked your mother, but I would never have killed her. Christ, what's got into you? Why on earth would you go about murdering innocent women? They have *children*, Billy, do you understand? They have little boys and girls who are crying like you were, who are going through what you did. I'm sorry, but what you've done is absolutely despicable."

"Oh no. Oh fuck. It *wasn't* you?"

"No!"

"But Mr Spencer thought…"

I don't care what your creepy soldier thought, you bloody cretin. "Why are these men really here?"

"I think they know. What I did. I think…"

God help me, but I'm going to throw him to the dogs. He's been a pest ever since he came to live with us. I can't have him bleating about this to anyone else.

He switched to the cajoling man he'd once been, when he'd spoken to Billy through the letterbox, coaxing information out of him to use against Emma. "Where are you, son?"

"Why do you need to know?"

Peter made eye contact with Ginger to let him know he was on their side. "So I can come and get you when I've got rid of these men. We'll figure something out. Hide you. Get you therapy so you don't do this again." He shook his head at his visitors to show he hadn't meant that.

"It won't work," Billy whined.

Anger surged. "Tell me where you are, boy," Peter shouted.

"I'm sorry…"

The line went dead.

"I tried," Peter said, Ginger and Blond glaring at him. "You heard me, didn't you? Is that why you're here, because of him? Because he…he…" He feigned retching and bent over. "Oh my God, I can't get my head around this." He sank down and sat on the cold step. "My son is the *Slasher*?"

"Where do you think he'd go?" Ginger hauled Peter to his feet and pushed his back against the doorjamb.

The wood dug into Peter's spine and hurt. "I don't know. Other than his house, I don't *know*."

"You'd better not be lying."

Blond stepped closer. "If we find out ye are and that ye killed his mother, we'll be back for ye, understand?"

Peter nodded. "It wasn't me. Billy…he's messed up in the head from seeing her being killed. I had nothing to do with it. He knows how much I disliked her and has got it into his head that it must have been me."

"Ye'd better not have done it. Who's Mr Spencer?"

"A stupid toy soldier he's had since he was little."

Blond took a card out of his pocket and put it in Peter's sweaty hand. "If he gets hold of ye again, ring us on that number—unless ye want another visit from the pigs."

Peter's teeth chattered. How did they know about that? Had they been watching his house all night?

"I just want him caught," he said. "What he's done…I can never forgive him. Those poor women…"

Ginger picked at his beard. It came away from his face with a blunted Velcro sound, and Blond did the same with his. Peter stared, flabbergasted. They tugged at their hair and put it in their pockets. Wigs. Blond spun his baseball cap around one finger. Peter gawped at two men he'd *never* wanted to meet. And it *had* to be them, didn't it?

The Brothers.

"I see you recognise us," Not-So-Ginger-Anymore said. "I'm George, and this is Greg. Now you know we *really* mean it when we say we'll be back if you've fucked us over. Billy is ours, he'll be *sorted*, and if you want to keep your nose clean, you'll let us know if he tells you where he is. He's got his sights on a woman tonight, we've seen him watching her, and if she ends up dying, *you'll* pay the price. And keep your gob shut about this. You tell no one, got it?" He smiled. "Have a nice night."

They stalked off to a BMW Peter hadn't clocked, one he *should* have clocked if he'd checked the camera before opening the door. They got in and drove away.

Peter pissed himself, hot fluid coasting down his legs, and he panted to catch his breath. Billy was a liability, one who could get him caught for what he'd done all those years ago. Son or not, if The Brothers 'sorting' him meant the secret remained safe, then that was what would happen. And no, he wouldn't be telling *anyone* about this.

He couldn't stand the humiliation of Michaela and Darren knowing who he really was. Getting older had shown him what his priorities should be, not to mention his wife having that stroke shitting the life out of him. He wanted to live out his days in peace, Emma far behind him, *and* her mosquito of a son, too.

Ashamed he'd wet himself, he went inside, taking off his soaked shoes, socks, and trousers. He put them in the washing machine on a hot cycle and headed for the shower, all the puzzle pieces slotting into place. Sheldon asking about Billy's hobby—the dumb bastard must have used other people's cars to abduct the women. Billy not answering his phone of an evening when Peter had phoned him from their holiday destinations—what had he been doing, stalking?

Peter had thought he'd taught his boy to hide his stupidity lately, but evidently, he hadn't. What an utterly silly prat to have reenacted his mother's murder—*four* times—especially if he'd written the same words on her chest and had carved a snake into her stomach. Would someone from Emma's case still be working at the station and eventually remember those things?

Fear for his own freedom coursed through Peter, and he cried beneath the water, wishing he'd never seen Emma and that little boy in town, alerting him to the fact he had a son with her. Wished his ego hadn't pushed him into claiming the child. Wished he hadn't wanted to hurt Emma by taking him away from her. If he'd been oblivious, none of this would be happening, and he wouldn't have the burden of an offspring who didn't know how to cover his tracks like his old man did.

God, the shame of it.

Chapter Twenty-Two

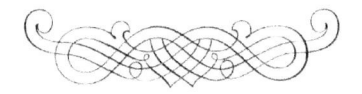

Greg sat in the driver's seat, having picked up on the fact George was too wired to drive. The last thing they needed was him streaking through the streets in the BMW, of all things, something they were known for, the police pulling them over. Another bite on the arse, what with Billy getting away from them, really wasn't on Greg's to-do list, and he doubted it was on

George's, who'd be steaming inside at him getting away.

When George had peeled his beard off, Greg had almost muttered, "About time." Acting as two thugs after money hadn't been getting them anywhere, and Peter was the type to only listen when it was clear he had no choice—trumped-up prick. Being presented with The Brothers had changed the dynamics, and Peter would now watch his back and steer clear of Billy if he knew what was good for him.

"What next?" Greg asked.

George grimaced. "We cruise until we find him."

"Doubtful he's just going to walk around in plain sight since he knows someone's after him. You heard him, he's hiding, and Peter let him know we were there."

"In plain sight? Have you *seen* this fucking fog or do you need to go to Specsavers?" George gestured out of the window at the thickening peasouper. "It's like the fates are on his side and want him to get away with it. Stop us from catching up with him. I swear Mum usually helps us out from up there, but she hasn't done it this time."

Greg scoffed. "Since when have you believed in fate, for fuck's sake?"

"Bog off."

Greg sighed. "Did you believe him? Peter?"

"What, that he didn't kill Billy's mum? The jury's out on that one. Without knowing all the ins and outs…"

"We need to get hold of Janine so we know the score. Ring her. Put it on speaker. If he seems suss to her, we'll bring him in."

George dialled her number. Greg hoped his brother didn't alienate Janine at this stage of the game. They needed her intel, and if George waded in like he usually did, he wouldn't blame her if she put the phone down on them.

"What have you two gone and done?" Janine asked. "If you've fucked things up by going to Peter Ford's house…"

She gritted her teeth, tired from doing overtime, and she *still* sat at her desk, going through the files regarding Clarke visiting Peter about his employee's death. If Clarke and Peter were good buddies at that time, which she believed they were, then it was plausible Peter could have asked him to bump Emma off. Why ask a copper, though?

He must have known he was bent.

All she'd come up with was that Clarke had spoken to the other members of staff. Stephanie Rogers had been kicked to death in her home one night, and her coworkers had alibis—all of them had been out together on a pub crawl. While they'd been in The Lion, in close proximity to Stephanie's house, it didn't mean they'd had anything to do with it. Witnesses had seen them drinking and being loud, and no one could recall them leaving to commit the murder then returning.

A quick poke into Stephanie's background didn't reveal any link between her and Peter other than he was her boss. Janine was satisfied he hadn't killed her, but she wasn't so sure he was innocent regarding the Emma business.

"Are you going to answer me or what?" she snapped.

"Shut up and listen," George said.

She bristled, but he sounded too agitated for her to bite back with a snarky comment. Despite being knackered and well able to shoot off a spiteful response, she knew when to cut her losses. "Okay…"

"What do you know about Billy's mother being murdered?"

Janine explained as much as she knew. "Why?"

"Because when we paid Peter a visit, he rang Billy to find out where he was for us, and Billy seemed to think Peter had killed her."

Janine's stomach lurched. "What?"

"Peter denied it, and he sounded genuine enough there, but he's had a lot of years to perfect his reaction. Seems Billy's killing those women because he thinks his dad killed his mother. Some fucked-up reasoning."

"He admitted it? Billy, I mean."

"Yep. Said he wanted his dad's help to stop him doing it."

"So he's got a conscience at least."

"Maybe, or he twigged we were all watching him tonight and he knows it's the end of the line. Peter tried to serve him up to us on a platter, so all isn't well in Ford land."

"Where is he now? Billy."

"No clue." George told her what had happened at The Angel.

"Shit, so even with all you lot there, he got away?" She couldn't resist that snipe. George claimed they were shit-hot, and she had pleasure in pointing out they weren't. Childish, but she wouldn't change for all the tea in China. Then she cursed the clubgoers for wanting to have a good time. "If that queue hadn't been there…"

"I know, and The Angel was packed. We couldn't get out quickly enough. Ichabod was near the door, but that Marlborough bint stopped him from leaving. Katy."

Janine frowned. "Are you saying she's in with Billy and blocked the way on purpose?"

"No, she's got a thing about Ichabod and won't leave him alone. We'd already carted her away from him earlier in the evening. It was just an unfortunate coincidence that she walked up to Ichabod when he was about to go after Billy. He was closest to the door and would have reached him if she hadn't done that."

"I like the way you call it an unfortunate coincidence when it's *your* fuck-up, but if it'd been me, you'd be down on me like a ton of bricks."

"My prerogative." George sniffed. "And don't think I didn't hear that barb earlier. I'll admit, we didn't plan it too well. Didn't realise the pub would be so busy, but with Debbie lowering her food prices, it was inevitable she'd get more custom."

"That's unlike you to admit when you're wrong."

"I'm still learning to do that, so cut me some slack."

"What are you doing now?"

"We've got people at The Angel. Debbie and Lillibet will kip upstairs in the flat tonight instead of going back to her place, so if he's still hanging about, watching, we'll have men nearby to collar him."

"But the fog might be an issue," Greg said. "Have you seen how bad it's got?"

"Hang on." Janine left her office. She walked to the window in the incident room and lifted the blind. "Oh. Shit. Well, good luck finding him in *that*. Maybe leave it for another day." She realised what she'd said and backtracked. "Actually, don't. If he doesn't get hold of Lillibet, he might go after someone else like he did with Sharny."

"I was gonna say," George grumbled, "*how* unfeeling did you just sound?"

"I wasn't thinking. I'm tired. I've pulled a double shift."

"So have we, so sorry, no pity party for you. No news from the coppers outside Billy's house, I take it?"

"Nope, not that they'll be able to see much."

"Same goes for our men at Lillibet's. We've heard nothing from them."

"You're absolutely certain no one saw him going up the steps to Debbie's flat?"

George grunted. "He ran down the back of the pub, must have vaulted the fence into the cemetery, but now you've said that, you've got me worried. I'll get someone to go and check her place is secure, but with the steel doors she's got and the amount of locks, I doubt anyone could get in."

"Okay, keep me posted if something happens."

"What's the score on Peter? You said your theory is he arranged for Emma to be killed by Clarke. Do we go and pick him up?"

Janine thought about that. Emma's murder had been so long ago, and as the file didn't specify the words written or the snake, she could get away with him being sorted by the twins, but… "Leave him for now. We've got the issue of the former DI who now knows about the carvings."

"Wonderful. So Peter could get away with it."

"No, after the Slasher shit is sorted, leave a bit of time to go by, then you could plough into him, make it look like a hit-and-run."

"Fine. Do you want Billy's body?"

"That would be nice, but it can't be left with a note like before. There's the general consensus here that we have a vigilante on our hands, conveniently delivering bodies for us to find, and I'm worried it's looking like the vigilante is getting inside info—from me. And you were mentioned last time, that it could be you two."

"Bollocks to that."

"I steered them away from that line of thought, but you get why we need to be careful." Taking her own advice, she walked out into the corridor to make sure no one had been listening. Despite the time, other coppers would be around. She stepped back into the incident room and shut the door. Leaned on it. "If you give him to me, make it seem like he was killed by a sex worker he tried to attack, so dump him in a known soliciting spot."

"That limits what I can do to him," George grumped. "A woman wouldn't do half the shit I've got planned."

"For once, hold Mad George in check. And don't put Billy on the rack. Jim's mentioned how the wounds on the backs of the others were all the same."

"Right, leave it with us."

She stared at her silent burner and stuffed it in her pocket. She'd forgotten to ask them why she hadn't been called in to help with the surveillance at The Angel, then decided she didn't care. In her office, she shut her computer down and packed up. After signing out of the station, she walked to her car, torch on, and nodded to Cameron parked on the street as she drove past him. The poor sod must have been bored shitless.

She took the journey slowly, the fog swirling in places, and didn't envy the twins trying to find Billy in this mess. She should have written a report on what Billy had admitted to his father, but how could she get around the fact George had told her? No, she'd have to let this pan out. She now worried that Peter might open his mouth and tell the police what his son had confessed to him.

At home, with Cameron heating up some microwave dinners and making sarnies to go with them, she messaged the twins.

JANINE: PF NEEDS A REMINDER NOT TO MENTION WHAT BILLY ADMITTED.

GG: DON'T WORRY ABOUT IT. WE WARNED HIM TO KEEP HIS TRAP SHUT. HE DIDN'T SAY IT IN FRONT OF YOU, AND AS FAR AS ANYONE'S CONCERNED, IF PETER RINGS THE OLD BILL EVEN THOUGH WE TOLD HIM NOT TO, IT'LL BE NEWS TO YOU. ACT LIKE IT IS ANYWAY.

JANINE: RIGHT. AGAIN, I'M NOT THINKING STRAIGHT. I SHOULD HAVE KNOWN YOU'D HAVE SORTED THAT.

With no response, she deleted the messages and sat at the table to eat macaroni cheese with a ham sandwich on the side. "Sorry about tonight. Me telling you not to follow me."

Cameron shrugged. "You know I hate doing that. What was it all about?"

"Where I went, you'd have been seen, the fog wasn't too bad by then, and I couldn't risk it. Suspect's house, other officers present."

"Ah, right."

She told him everything else between bites of food, and he agreed with her that Billy's body needed to be delivered without the usual note and telltale signs he'd been hoisted onto the rack.

"People will start getting suspicious," he said, "and you don't deserve to get nicked for working for the twins."

Sometimes, though, she thought she did.

Chapter Twenty-Three

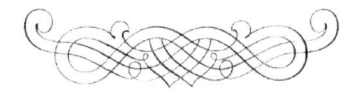

Lillibet and Debbie had stayed for a lock-in at The Angel with Jimmy and Ichabod. George had messaged to say they had to sleep in Debbie's flat tonight, something about the journey back to Lillibet's being unnecessary and dangerous, not only because of the fog but Billy was on the loose. He wasn't at her house, or his, and he wasn't with his father, although George couldn't be certain of that. Peter had taken a while to answer the front door to them, so he could have been ushering Billy upstairs and coaching him on what to say when he phoned him.

That didn't settle Lillibet's nerves any.

George had said he wished they'd gone into Peter's house and searched it at the time, so they were returning there and doing that now. Alien and Brickhouse had been sent home but then brought back out—one currently stood on Kitchen Street, the other on Debbie's Corner in case Billy chose another woman. Several men from the twins' camp had positioned themselves at other soliciting areas, keeping to the shadows and watching who turned up to proposition the women, noting all license plates. Billy might have a second car, although Janine had passed on that only a Merc SUV was in his name and that he must be using fake plates.

Police officers sat outside Billy's house. Maxwell and Nate were at hers. While it seemed all avenues had been covered, Lillibet still had doubts. If Billy was out on the streets, he could wait it out, smash the security light in The Angel's car park, and break into Debbie's flat while they slept, despite all the locks. Yes, Will was outside in his car, but what if Billy tampered with the light when everyone left The Roxy? Will wouldn't see him behind the crowds of people leaving the nightclub and the fog obscuring his view.

"I'm knackered," Debbie said. "I think we should turn in."

A stupid thing to worry about in the circumstances, but Lillibet hadn't brought an overnight bag with her. The change of plan had unnerved her, as had Billy getting away. Why had he left the pub? Had he realised people were watching him? Or was it like Janine had said when she'd rung half an hour ago? His father had got spooked after she'd visited him and warned Billy to leave, which meant Peter knew all about what his son was up to.

She thought about her old boss. He didn't seem the type to condone murder, even if it was his lad committing it. His business dealings had been straight down the line, no subterfuge, and he coveted being known as an honest man. Unless that was a front to hide what was going on behind the scenes.

Too many questions floated around Lillibet's mind, and she didn't think she'd get a wink of sleep, although her body ached, as did her head. She rose from the bar stool and stooped to pick up her bag, pausing at the sound of sirens.

"Oh God," Debbie said. "Has he abducted one of my girls on the corner?"

They all rushed to the exit at once, Jimmy getting there first. He unlocked it, drew the bolts across, and flung the double doors open. The fog now had a friend—thick billows of grey smoke that chuntered down the street. Jimmy stepped outside, followed by Ichabod.

Debbie clutched Lillibet's hand. "Stay with me. We're going to my flat no matter what's going on out there, okay?"

Fear groped Lillibet's heart with sticky fingers, and she felt sick. She moved outside with Debbie. People emerged from the fog, running, their faces smeared with terror. With vision limited, she only caught sight of those closest to her, and they appeared in a nightmarish stream of panicked chaos, mouths open, eyes wide.

"What's going on?" Debbie shouted to whoever would listen.

"The Roxy's on fire," a bloke yelled, then the fog scoffed him up.

"Shit." Debbie held Lillibet's hand tighter and pushed through the unseen melee ahead.

Where were Jimmy and Ichabod?

"Get to the flat, now!" Jimmy's disembodied voice floated for a moment, then a loud boom and screeches drowned it out.

Had Billy set the fire as a distraction?

No, he can't want to kill me that much, can he? I'm no one.

She followed Debbie through the murk, the air tasting of smoke. It caught in the back of her throat, and she coughed, her eyes watering. Someone barrelled out of the fog, shoving between them, Debbie's hand breaking away. Anxiety surged inside Lillibet, and she staggered to the side, bumping into what she thought must be the wall of The Angel.

"Lillibet?" Debbie called.

A hand clasped Lillibet's and, calmed now her friend had found her, she let herself be led away. Debbie walked fast, and Lillibet stumbled, trying to keep up.

"Wait, I can't see anything," she said.

Muted by the noise of people shouting, talking, and screaming, a car door release blipped. Had they made it into the car park and

Debbie planned to drive them away from here? Debbie let go of her hand and pushed her shoulders. Lillibet shot forward, her palms landing on a back seat, and she scrambled inside, relieved to be safer. An almighty wallop to the crown of her head sent pain spearing into her brain, and she cried out, slumping.

The vague thought registered that Debbie wouldn't have done that to her, it had to have been someone else's hand she'd held.

Then nothing.

Chapter Twenty-Four

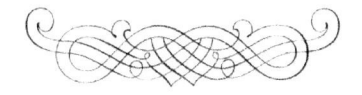

The morning sun woke Billy as it crept around the edges of his bedroom curtains. He'd had a horrible dream about Mummy being hurt, a man called Mr Black cutting her. There had been so much blood, and Billy hadn't rung the police or anything. He'd just stood there and watched it all. Glad it had only been a dream, he found Mr Spencer under his pillow and took him to Mummy's room. Her door was shut, so he

opened it, getting ready to dive on her bed and wake her up to ask her why she hadn't come in last night to give him a kiss.

He made it two steps, the floor creaking, then stopped.

The blood wasn't red now but brown, and Mummy was still there, her eyes closed. The shock of it all being real brought tears to Billy's itchy eyes, and he staggered over to the bed and climbed on. Something wet soaked into his bare knees. The blood.

He ignored it and stared at her. If he woke her up, she'd be okay then. She'd tell him what to do to fix the cuts, and everything would be all right.

The wind chime tinkled.

Something didn't smell nice. Was it the blood?

He poked her arm, and it was stiff beneath the end of his finger. "Mummy?"

Did the yellow cloth just move in her mouth, or had he imagined it?

"Mummy?"

His tears fell, hot on his cheeks, and he stared at her belly. The blood had been wiped away, her skin was cleaner than last night, and he tried to make out what Mr Black had done. Was that a picture of a snake?

The urgency to get help finally blasted into him, and he shot off the bed, stumbling his way out of the room.

He sped downstairs, Mr Spencer's arm digging into his palm where he held him so tightly. He went to the phone on the little table in the hallway but didn't pick it up. Kelsie would know what to do. He reached for the Yale handle and pulled it down. Opened the door. He ran outside and along the street, small stones digging into his feet, the cold biting at his legs. He'd forgotten he'd taken his pyjama bottoms off when he'd wet himself. Up Kelsie's path, and he stretched for the bell push, poking it in. A ding-dong *echoed inside.*

Kelsie's mum opened the door. "What are you doing out here dressed like that, *Billy?"*

"Mummy…Mummy…"

"Shit, what's happened?"

"Mummy…she won't wake up."

"Get inside. Go up to Kelsie, tell her I said she has to watch you."

Billy went in and ran upstairs, promising himself he'd never speak again after he'd told Kelsie what her mum had said. If he did, Mr Black might find out and come back.

<hr />

Hannah Bishop didn't like the sound of this, nor the fact Billy didn't have any pyjama bottoms on. Or that his knees had scuffs of blood on them. Where had it come from?

Nervous, she marched to Emma's house, the door wide open, and quickly went inside. She checked the living room in case Emma was on the sofa, then took the stairs, out of breath by the time she got to the top. The faint stench of copper pennies hit her, and she eased along the landing, a pool of dread swirling in her stomach. At Emma's bedroom door, she stared and knew exactly where that blood had come from. Billy must have knelt on the bed as a large patch had soaked into the quilt. Depending on when this had happened, it might still be wet in the fibres beneath the brown top layer.

"Oh, Emma love… I told you it was dangerous to earn money like that…"

Hannah didn't go in. It was obvious the woman was dead. The shock of this had kept the full force of fear at bay to begin with, but it paid a visit now, and the enormity of the situation caught up with her. Terrified the killer was still there, she ran downstairs and out onto the street, catching sight of Marge over the road about to get in her car.

"Wait!" Hannah wheezed, lumbering up to her. "I need to use your phone."

Marge frowned, her grey hair tousled by the breeze. "But your house is just there."

"I know, but Billy's in with Kelsie, and I don't want him hearing me."

Marge dipped a hand in her bag and took her mobile out. She handed it over. "Whatever's gone on?"

"It's Emma, she's dead." Hannah jabbed the nine three times.

"What?"

Hannah flapped a hand to shut her up; the person on the other end had answered. "Police, please. My neighbour's been killed."

Marge flumped against the side of her car while Hannah continued speaking, answering questions as best she could with the limited knowledge she had. It seemed to take an age for the police car to arrive, followed by an ambulance that wouldn't be needed, but maybe that was for them to check if Emma really was dead.

"They're here," Hannah said to the dispatcher.

"Okay, you can end the call now."

Hannah did that and gave the phone back to Marge who'd gone a bit pale. Hannah didn't have time to pander to the street's hypochondriac, although in this case she felt bad for thinking that as the news must have been a shock.

She dashed over to the police getting out of their car, pointing to Emma's house. "She's in there."

The PCs nodded and went in.

Another car arrived, a plain one, and two suited men emerged onto the pavement.

"I'm the one who found her," Hannah blurted. "Her son's in my house. He…he came to me and said she wouldn't wake up. She's been stabbed in the neck, and someone's written 'lying bitch' on her. Looks like it was with a knife."

"Oh God," Marge muttered.

The tall copper held up some ID. "DI Neil Zeller and DS Rod Clarke. And you are?"

"Hannah. Hannah Bishop. I'm two doors down from Emma's."

"Talk to my colleague about what happened." Zeller went back to the car and poked about in the boot. He took something out in a transparent bag and wandered to the house.

Clarke must have clocked her frown. "He has to put gloves on and covers over his shoes. Evidence contamination." He seemed smug she didn't know and that he'd had to explain.

Twat. *"Right. I…I didn't touch anything, not even the front door because it was already open."*

"So what happened?" He smiled, revealing large, unsightly yellow teeth, and took a notebook and pen out of his suit jacket's inner pocket. His hair needed a wash, and he looked like he'd not long rolled out of bed. Or maybe that was just his style.

Hannah related everything. She ended with, "Her son...Emma said his father's Peter Ford who lives in that big house up Holston Way, the one with the half-circle steps out the front. But he doesn't know Billy's his, she never told him."

"Billy?"

"The son. He's only eight."

"Ah, well, that's a pisser, isn't it, losing his mum like that. Do you think he slept through it all?"

"How would I know? I didn't get the chance to speak to him properly."

Clarke took his phone out and wandered a few feet away. "Shall I see to the kid, boss?" He lowered his voice and turned his back.

Hannah faced Marge. "This is bloody awful."

Marge flapped a hand in front of her face, probably to cool her red cheeks. "You're telling me. There's been a man at Emma's door every night for the past few weeks."

"What?"

"He crouches and talks through the letterbox, or maybe he's just staring inside, I don't know."

"And you didn't tell *anyone?"*

Marge shrugged. "Not my place. You know I like to keep to myself."

"But Emma works at night and Billy's on his own."

*"*I *didn't know that, did I!"*

"You'll have to tell that copper."

Clarke came over. "Social services will be here shortly. We'll speak to Billy then. I take it he's with someone at the minute?"

"I told you, my daughter." Hannah glanced at Marge. "Tell him."

"Tell me what?" Clarke's eyebrows met in the middle.

Marge launched into her story, then added, "And before you ask, no, I didn't write the number plate of his car down, and no, I don't know what make it is, just that it's black."

"That could be anyone," Clarke muttered. "What did he look like?"

Marge rolled her eyes. "It's dark by the time he shows up, so no idea."

"Why didn't you speak to Emma about this?"

"Because I thought he was talking to her. *I didn't know she went out and left her son until Hannah just told me."*

Clarke swung his attention to Hannah. "She left *him?"*

"She's a prostitute. Was."

Marge gasped.

Clarke remained po-faced. "And where did she work?"

"On Julio Street."

He seemed uncomfortable.

"Is something wrong?" Hannah asked. Did he know Emma because of his job? Or…no, a copper wouldn't use a prosser, would they?

"No, no." Clarke smiled, although he appeared flustered. "Terrible business, this."

The arrival of two more police cars snatched Hannah's attention. Neighbours had come out and stood on doorsteps, some in their dressing gowns. The new officers came over to Clarke who instructed them to get on with house-to-house enquiries. He sent them off with a wave.

"I could murder a cuppa," he said to Hannah.

She didn't think murder was an appropriate word in the circumstances and said so.

"Figure of speech, slip of the tongue." Clarke grinned.

He wasn't right, something about him unnerved her, and she folded her arms.

"You can come to mine if you like," she said. "Marge, are you coming an' all?"

Marge nodded. "I was only off to the market. I need a sit down because of all this. Just dreadful."

You want the gossip, that's what you bloody want.

In Hannah's house, sitting around the kitchen table with the door shut so Billy couldn't hear them from upstairs, they drank their tea. Clarke asked a lot of personal questions about Emma, although he didn't write all of it down, which was strange.

The bell pealed, and Hannah stood.

"I'll go," Clarke said.

He left the room, and Marge gave Hannah one of her knowing looks.

"He's weird," Marge whispered. "Giving me the creeps, he is."

Hannah sat back down. "Same here. I can't put my finger on it, though."

"Me neither. I suppose he would *be interested in Emma. It's his job."*

"I know, but it feels more than that."

But what was it?

Clarke stood on the kitchen threshold. Zeller spoke to Billy at the table gently, trying to coax information out of him, as did the social worker. But the kid was silent. The shock of finding his mother, most likely. Kelsie had come down, too, and she'd said she couldn't get anything out of him either after he'd said she had to look after him.

Bloody good job an' all. The favour he'd done for Peter last night had been nerve-racking yet exhilarating, and he was a tad unnerved this morning in case he got caught. He'd worn gloves and a balaclava, but there was always the chance of transference, which was why he'd got internally wound up when Zeller had entered Emma's house alone. Clarke wanted to be in there so any hairs he might have left behind would be put down to an officer at the scene. He had to go inside somehow, couldn't risk not doing it.

He reckoned he'd done a good job when speaking to Hannah, feigning that he hadn't known who Billy was, but he'd been well aware Emma had a son and what he was called. When he'd walked into her bedroom last night he'd recognised her but couldn't for the life of him think where from. It hadn't been until Hannah had mentioned Julio Street and Emma being a prostitute that he'd twigged, and he could have brained Peter for not being more forthcoming with information. Clarke hadn't been able to check her out on the police database prior to killing her as it would have come up once the investigation into her death started and Zeller would want to know why he'd run a search previous to her murder.

Clarke used prostitutes often, and he'd been with Emma a few weeks back. When they'd first had sex, he'd told her he was a copper and that he'd dob her in if she didn't give him the goods for free; after that, he'd had two more blow jobs off her.

In her bedroom, after she'd died, he'd rooted through her handbag in the partially open drawer which had a lock on the front and a key on top. She'd been busy putting her bag in there when he'd crept out of her wardrobe where he'd been hiding for ages. He'd found money, a fair bit of it, and had stuffed it in his pocket.

He'd left the house promising himself that once this case was over—because he'd known he'd be called out with Zeller for this, they always were when it came to murder in this area of the East End—he'd never admit to himself he'd done this. He'd block it out, pretend he'd been at home in bed. Better that than recall it and accidentally put his foot in it later down the line.

The urge to shag her after he'd killed her had been strong, but in this instance he'd refrained, especially as he'd mangled her fanny and tits with the knife like Peter wanted. Leaving any pubic hairs would have got him right in the shit. He had ambitions to become a DI, someone to be reckoned with in the force, and no amount of sexual need could derail that.

I shouldn't have agreed to do this.

But Peter had been his best mate as kids, and the bloke was going out of his mind with worry over his son, although he had no proof Billy was his, and let's face it, Emma had slept with hundreds of men, so the lad could be anyone's. Emma hadn't sent in the DNA test Peter had arranged, and what with Billy being left every night for hours on end, Peter had been desperate.

Why didn't he tell me she was a prosser?

Clarke had warned Peter that Billy would be taken into care if Emma's family didn't want to welcome the boy in, and a test would be done to determine whether Peter was his father before he could look after him. Peter was prepared to do whatever it took to get his son, clearly, because otherwise, he wouldn't have asked Clarke to kill her.

It had been said in a jokey way at first, and Clarke had laughed it off, but it had become obvious, when they'd sat in a West End pub, that Peter wasn't joking. The money on offer had swayed Clarke, although he'd be paid cash in dribs and drabs because, of course, Peter's bank accounts would be scrutinised as he'd be a suspect—upset father hires hitman. He regularly drew large amounts of money out for his wife to spend willy-nilly, so it wouldn't look odd if he took out another couple of hundred a week. Clarke had worked out he'd receive the payments for a bloody long time until the agreed amount had been paid.

He'd be having words with Peter, though, for not telling him the full story. How Emma was a prosser. It meant the investigation would be a big one, loads of working girls to speak to, punters traced. Clarke didn't like having a lot of work on his plate, and if he'd known Emma's profession beforehand, he might have refused to do the deed.

Nah, ten grand is too much to turn down. I'd have done it anyway.

Zeller stood, drawing Clarke out of his thoughts.

"We'll be off for now." Zeller nodded to everyone and pointed at Clarke for him to go ahead of him down the hallway. Outside, he said, "You need to see the scene to believe it. Come on."

Clarke nodded, relieved.
Thank you, God.

Chapter Twenty-Five

Lillibet woke in an empty room. The grey carpet beneath her head smelled new, bits of fluff dotted about as if it had recently been fitted. White paint on the walls, the skirting board shiny from gloss. She glanced at the ceiling to the source of light, a crystal chandelier twinkling. The white panelled door seemed so far away, but she made out a keyhole. She sat up, her head banging, throbbing in time with her accelerating pulse. Another door, behind her. She'd try that.

She struggled to her feet, swaying, and turned the handle, nausea rising. A bathroom—so she was in a bedroom with an en suite? She stepped inside, the marble floor tiles gleaming. No shampoo or anything, no towels. One toilet roll. Despite her predicament, she needed the loo. She'd drunk a lot of lemonade over the course of the evening. Shaking, she did her business quickly, not wanting the shame of being caught in a private moment by whoever had shoved her into that car and brought her here.

Not being able to fill in the gap between then and now sent her nerves spiking. She flushed the toilet, rinsed her hands, then laughed wryly at ingrained habits emerging even though she'd found herself here, maybe kidnapped. She left the bathroom, walking to the other door, and banged on it.

"Debbie?" A hopeless wish, she knew that deep inside, but she *could* be in a spare room that Debbie hadn't got around to furnishing, couldn't she? "Deb?"

The sound of a key twisting in the lock had her springing back, her chest tightening. She retreated, half of her wanting to be as far away as she could from whoever entered, the other half wishing she'd stayed closer so she could lash out if it wasn't Debbie, Jimmy, Ichabod, or the twins. But if it *was* them, they'd have laid her on a bed, not a bare floor. If it was them, she wouldn't be locked in.

Billy slipped inside the small gap, closing the door. It took a moment for her to process him, to accept her situation. He *was* the Slasher, and she *was* on his list. There was no getting away from that now, no convincing herself Janine had got it all wrong.

"This was supposed to be our bedroom. I was getting it ready for when you moved in, but you decided to be a slag and ruin it all." He sighed, but it wasn't one of resignation, more that she'd pissed him off. "You gave me the right runaround tonight. Fucking hell, why did you have to make it so *difficult*?"

"What do you want with me?" she asked, knowing full well but playing this the best way she knew how. Stalling for time. Surely everyone would realise she wasn't outside The Angel anymore and people would be looking for her. Yes, it was foggy and smoky, but time had passed, and they'd know she hadn't made it to Debbie's flat or back to the bar in the pub.

"I want you dead, Mum."

Mum?

A chill swept over her. He was mad, he had to be.

"What?" she said. "I'm not your mum."

He cast his gaze over her from head to toe then sneered, his top lip curling so much his nostrils flared. He thought Lillibet was filthy? Used? Tainted? His expression said so much, more than words ever could.

"But you're like her," he said.

Goosebumps rose on her arms and sprouted all over her scalp. The ache in her head increased, on the crown where he'd hit her. What had he used? Had he been able to get something out of the boot of his car without Will seeing? A tyre iron? Had it broken the skin and bled? She reached up slowly to touch it, then brought her hand down to inspect her fingers.

Tacky blood.

Panic forced the words out of her mouth. "Please, can we talk about this?" She'd sounded too desperate and sensed she needed to remain calm with him.

"We already are."

"Why…why do you want me dead?"

"People like you, you make me sick."

"People like me?"

"Slags. Women who sell themselves. Don't you *know* how degrading that is? How it affects other people?" He leaned on the door. "My life was so fucked up because of what my mum did. It still is." He punched the side of his head. "I can't get it out of here. It's stuck, and he keeps telling me bad things about her, when I know she was good."

Who's he? Peter?

"Fucking bastard filled me with all those stories, but she was nice to me, she tried her best. Jesus Christ, I don't know what to *think* anymore. Mr Spencer says Dad killed her, but Dad says he didn't."

Mr Spencer?

"If you think she was good, then she must have been." Lillibet's heart fluttered, missing beats. "It was just a job she did. If it makes you feel any better, know it was likely just to get money, it wouldn't have meant anything else."

"Is that what it is for you?" He'd framed it as an accusation, not a query. As if he didn't believe her.

"Yes. I got into debt. I went out too much with the other girls from Fords'. They had cash floating around, they could afford it, but me and Pippa, we couldn't keep up."

"*She's* a slag, too, that Pippa."

"No, she isn't, she was roped into it by a man called Crook. He gave her money to clear her bills, and she had to sell herself to earn enough to pay him back. It was a mess, and she didn't have any choice."

"What about you? Did *you* make a choice, or did someone else do that for you? That Crook man?"

"I met him, and he told me he ran girls, but it was *my* decision. I worked nights while at Fords' during the day. It was only meant to be until I'd sorted myself out, but Debbie offered me the job of looking after the women, and it paid more than your dad did so…"

"So you must like it. Spreading your legs for perverts. My mum had no choice. She had a conviction so couldn't get another job, no one would hire her." He kicked back at the door. "If she hadn't got in trouble, she could have worked in a shop, anything other than what she did. *He said it's all her fault, that if she'd behaved like a normal woman, she wouldn't have had to be a tart."*

"She did what she could to feed you."

"Yes."

"Then why are you so angry about it? Why take it out on other women?"

"Because of *him*."

"Who?"

"My dad! I swear he killed Mum, but I'm confused. He was too big, and Mr Black was smaller."

Mr Black?

He punched his head again. "Fuck off! Get out! Get out!"

Is he talking to me?

Lillibet moved forward to leave like he'd asked, but he gripped her wrist.

"Not you. You stay here until I know what to do with you."

"Who were you telling to get out, then?"

"The words. His words. Fuck. Shit!" He thumped his temple, eyes scrunched shut.

Lillibet took the opportunity to knee him in the bollocks. He pitched forward, bending over, although he didn't let her wrist go, tightening his hold instead.

"You fucking *bitch*! I was going to be nice if you promised to live here with me, but you *ruined* it again." He stood upright and, tears streaming down his cheeks, launched a right hook at her.

She staggered to the side from the force and landed on her arse on the floor. Then he was on her, pinning her down, his face contorted in a nasty sneer.

"You're going to regret that. You're just like her, a dirty slapper."

He wrenched at her blouse, snatching at it, but the buttons held. She struck his face, raked her nails down it, fighting to get him off her, but he sat up on her chest, grabbed her hands one at a time, and pinned them beneath his knees. Out of breath, he glared down at her.

"I don't want to do this anymore, but I have to."

She stilled, sensing this was a pivotal moment. If she played it right, he might still let her go. "You don't have to do it. No one needs to know it was you who took me. We can go out, a few dates or whatever, like you wanted. We can talk through everything, work out how you can stop doing this."

"I *can't* stop, not now."

"Why not? You're the Slasher, but the police don't know who you are, so…"

"How do you know who I am?" He seemed genuinely bewildered.

Is he off his rocker?

"It's obvious, you brought me here, but we can keep it a secret. I'll help you."

"No you won't. As soon as you're out of here, you'll go to the coppers."

"I thought we were friends," she lied. It didn't take much to force tears out. She was shit-scared and desperate to get away from him.

"But you said no to dates."

"*Debbie* said no, not me. I said not at the minute, remember?" She struggled to draw air in. "I can't breathe properly, Billy. Can you get off me?"

He studied her, contemplating, and it was so clear something rolled around in his head, questions, options, and whether or not to believe her. He stuck a hand in his pocket and brought out a knife, although it appeared as a handle until he pressed a button and a blade popped out. Her whole body turned cold, and she couldn't stop staring at it. Was it the same one he'd used on Sharny and the other women?

He shifted back to settle on her stomach. The move meant her hands were freed, and she raised them, joining them together in a prayer—she wanted to hit him, but she had to gain his trust. Had to go against every instinct that screamed inside her.

"Please don't hurt me. I swear, this *will* be a secret between us. I'll never tell anyone who you are."

"I can't risk it." He shuddered. "I'm not going to mark your cheeks, I don't want to wreck your pretty face, but as for the rest…"

He used the knife to cut her blouse near each button, the fabric falling to the sides to expose her bra-covered breasts. She'd been with countless men for money, and when she'd slept around for fun, but *she'd* been in control then, and showing off her chest had been a part of the transaction. Now, it felt obscene, and embarrassing, and so *wrong*. A violation. Once again, emotions brought on by someone else ransacked her, and the sudden urge to hurt him, *really hurt him*, savaged her. She held it back, though it was difficult, and looked him in the eyes.

"It doesn't have to be like this," she said. "Where are we? At your house? Think of the evidence, how you can't deny I was here if the police work out it's you. There'll be blood, and they'll *know*."

He flinched, perhaps fighting whatever war raged inside him, but her words hadn't registered. She could tell by the set of his jaw and the weird blankness that had shuttered his eyes.

He put the point of the knife to her chest.

And carved.

Chapter Twenty-Six

What the serpent on Emma's stomach meant, Clarke had no chuffing idea, but he was gunning to find out. A week had passed since he'd killed Emma, and he'd met Peter in the West End again tonight, a small pub, The Golden Lion, packed to the gills. Both on the whiskey, they sat in a corner, Clarke with his back to the other customers. He just had to hope no one he knew came in and saw him, although he could *say he'd agreed to chat to Peter about the ordeal, that the bloke needed someone to offload to. He'd have to file that at the station, but it'd be plausible. Regardless, he didn't want the hassle.*

"Any news?" Peter asked.

"It's a dead end as to who the killer is if that's what you're getting at."

"But what about me?"

"You have a solid alibi and your bank accounts have come back clean. We planned it that way, didn't we, so unless Zeller wants to keep poking, you're safe."

"Billy's coming to us tomorrow. The test results came back. He's mine."

Clarke rolled his eyes. "Obviously, else he wouldn't be on his way to you, would he."

"Christ, why are you always so sarcastic?"

"Dunno. I like it. So you've got his room all done up, then?"

"Yes. Michaela's been out and bought him clothes and whatnot. Darren's excited to meet him. Michaela's finally got over the fact I cheated on her and is looking forward to having a new son—I suspect it's so she doesn't have to have another herself. I wanted two kids, but after having Darren, she swore she wouldn't do it again. It's a win-win all round."

"How the fuck did you get away with her accepting you'd played the field and had a child by a slapper?"

Peter chuckled. "I blamed it on her. Said if she'd been a bit more attentive in the bedroom, I wouldn't have strayed. You know how it is because you do it yourself: if we don't get what we need at home, we go elsewhere. Michaela's never been one for the kinky stuff, so I go to women who are."

"Why marry her if she isn't into that type of shit?"

"Her father's money." Peter sighed. "I also pointed out to her that I provide a damn good life and it seemed once we'd got married she went off the boil. She turned bright red, so I'd hit the nail on the head."

That would really bug Clarke. Damned if he'd put up with that. Mind you, if he had a woman as pretty as Michaela, he'd force *her to have sex with him the way he wanted. You didn't buy the whole cow and not eat it, did you. "Doesn't that piss you off?"*

Peter's forehead scrunched. "What do you mean?"

"That she used you because she knew you'd make loads of money?"

Peter shrugged. "It did at first, but the fact I can manipulate her all the time now to do whatever I want, well, I'm not turning that opportunity down."

Clarke laughed. "A man after my own heart. I bet you click your fingers and she jumps."

"If she wants money to spend, she'll have to. Seems she's prepared to do that."

"Shallow bitch."

"Hmm. She's like me. Out for herself. So long as she turns a blind eye when I have my affairs in future, and she looks after Billy, her lifestyle is safe."

"And if she doesn't?"

"That's where you come in."

Clarke shook his head. "Fuck right off. I'm not getting rid of another one for you."

"I was joking."

But was he? Clarke didn't think so.

Sod this for a game of soldiers.

"You keep your head down and play the good father," Clarke said to change the subject. "If I know Zeller, he'll be waiting for you to slip up. Yes, you're officially off the list because of your alibi and nothing funny going on with your finances, but he's like a dog with a missing bone and tends to keep digging."

Peter sighed. "I'll pay you another five grand if you steer him in a different direction."

Clarke wasn't averse to taking money under the table, providing he'd never get caught. He liked having readies he could spend on whatever he wanted—prossers and booze. He regularly took backhanders from scrotes who committed crime and fucked about with evidence if he had to—bent coppers were everywhere, and he just happened to be one of them.

"Fine by me," he said. "But wait a few months before you start upping the payments to cover that. Best to be safe. Zeller's retiring next year, so hopefully the case will go cold." He sipped some whiskey. "Why didn't you tell me Emma was a prosser?"

"I didn't think it was relevant."

"It is when it means the workload triples because of all the people we've had to speak to. I don't like too much work, and I've been run off my feet."

"Are you saying if you'd known, you wouldn't have done it?"

"No, I'm just making a point. So, the serpent. What's the deal with that?"

Peter smiled. "Deception. Slyness. And that forked tongue—Emma had one from time to time, so it seemed fitting."

"That's a bit deep."

"I can be. Why did you ask?"

"It's driving Zeller mad, the significance."

"Then tell him you've been thinking about it and you reckon you know what it means. Brownie points an' all that."

"Hmm, but it might steer the investigation back to you. She deceived you about Billy. Zeller will twig that in a heartbeat."

"Keep it to yourself, then." Peter got up. "Another round?"

"Why not."

While he was gone, Clarke stared at the wall and listened to the chatter around him. Posh cunts and their brand of humour naffed him off, mainly because he hadn't been born with a silver spoon up his arse. That annoyed him something chronic, that he wasn't who he wanted to be, someone who had endless money to burn and didn't have to work because Daddy was rich. Billy and Darren would have a life like that. Peter's business raked in the cash, the bloke was loaded, and Clarke was oddly pleased he'd played a part in giving Billy a whole new world. He'd get to watch him grow up, live the life Clarke had always wanted. See who he would have become in Billy's shoes.

Peter came back and put their glasses down, then sat. "Someone at the bar was talking about Emma's murder, saying they think her son's father did it. How I didn't say anything, I don't know. I wanted to punch their lights out."

"Not a good idea."

"I know, which is why I left them to it. How many others think it was me? What if Zeller hears about the gossip and dives in for another look at me?"

"Don't sweat it. Like we just agreed, I'll steer him elsewhere. Maybe frame that fella, if we eventually find him."

"What, the one who said he'd given her an extra fifty quid?"

"Yeah. You did well there, by the way. Came off as a concerned father visiting her place to make sure Billy was okay and you saw that man off. Not sure Zeller bought the fact the bloke exists, though. If neighbours had seen him, too, then maybe he'd believe it, but…"

"Are you deliberately winding me up, trying to worry me?"

Yep. That control you like…I like it, too. *"Nope, just keeping you in the loop like you asked me to."*

"Because I was going to say…"

"I could make out that when that Marge woman said she saw you every night, that it was him. You know, a stalker who spoke to Billy through the letterbox."

"But what if Billy decides to speak about it all? Okay, he's been mute since it happened, but he'll talk eventually."

"Then you do what you do best and manipulate him into saying what you want him to. You've already been doing it on the nightly visits. The groundwork's done, you just have to build the house. But make sure it isn't made of cards and can come tumbling down, for fuck's sake. I'm not getting in the shit for you."

"Grooming Billy to believe what I want will be easy. Look at Darren and how he is. And Michaela."

"Your own little army of people obeying you."

Peter smiled. "That's how it should be."

Clarke laughed to hide his envy. He'd love people to do whatever he wanted. "Got any pointers on that score?"

Peter smiled. "See, here's how it's done…"

Chapter Twenty-Seven

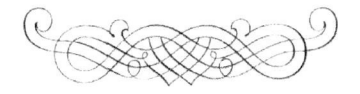

The faint, muted scream coming from inside Billy's house galvanised George into action. Standing out the back, where they'd crept in the fog to avoid the coppers out the front from seeing them, parking in the street behind, he hurriedly used the lock pick on the door. In a forensic suit, gloves, and mask, he pushed it open and got his bearings. A kitchen. Modern. White glossy cabinets, light glowing from the ones on the wall. No one in sight.

He ran through into a wide square hallway then poked his head into another room—a lounge, the TV on but the volume low. He followed the sound of another scream, although it was muffled, as if a hand covered a mouth—he'd heard that enough times to know he was right. He prayed the coppers didn't get wind of anything going on, but they were in a car, so unlikely.

He took the stairs two at a time, sensing Greg behind him, and opened door after door on the long landing. All of them led to bedrooms and one bathroom, which left one closed.

Another scream, and he twisted the doorknob, careful to be quiet. He inched his head around the edge and assessed the scene. A man sitting on a woman, his back to George. He recognised Lillibet's blouse, the fabric ruched down by her side. And blood dripping towards her armpit, the crude carving of an L just visible on her chest.

The start of Lying Bitch?

Jesus fuck.

George turned to Greg behind him and made a stabbing motion to convey a blade was being used, then shook his head at Greg's silent question: *Is she dead?* George faced frontwards again and took his gun out, moving the door bit by bit, sneaking in. He reached Lillibet's feet, and she opened her eyes, catching sight of him standing taller than Billy's head. George put a finger to his lips, then in one swift move, he gripped Billy's shirt at the back of his neck, jammed the business end of the gun to his temple, and hauled him off her.

Billy shouted in shock, arms flailing, the knife tip coming perilously close to George's face. A quick punch to the side of the bastard's head from Greg sent the bloke out of George's grip and to the floor. Before Billy had time to leap up and defend himself, George was on him, kicking him in the dick. Billy screeched.

Now curled on his side and in pain, he held his groin, and George wanted to shoot him in the fucking head, obliterate the brain that told this wanker it was okay to kill innocent women, but he held back one of his personalities, Mad, the side of him who didn't listen to reason, remembering what Janine had asked him to do.

Make it look like Billy had been killed by a sex worker.

George snatched at Billy's shirt and dragged him to his feet, pressing the gun to the side of his head again as a warning to play ball. Greg went to Lillibet and helped her up. The blood on the carpet would be a problem, the police would come here once Billy's body was found, and they'd know someone else had been here, too.

"Got any reason to have your DNA on record?" he asked Lillibet, aware he should have checked if she was all right first, although the word LYING on her chest was a good indication she wasn't. That must have hurt, even though the cuts were shallow.

"No," she said, that one word shaking out of her mouth, her body joining the tremble party.

She gripped Greg's forensic suit, and he held her tightly to his side, stroking her hair. Much as George was touched by the scene, how his brother's main focus was on the poor cow in his arms, someone needed a clear head.

"Get hold of the clean-up crew," he said. "This carpet needs to be dumped. Make them aware coppers are out the front and they'll need to use the back."

"What if the blood's gone through to the floor underneath?" Greg asked.

"Then we'll just have to hope Lillibet doesn't get in any trouble for them to match the blood to her in future."

"I won't," she said. "I'm leaving, I can't stay here now. I can't…"

George got it. She'd want to distance herself from this as much as she could.

"And as for you…" He jabbed the gun harder into Billy's temple, wishing he hadn't because it might leave a bruise or mark. "You're lucky I'm not allowed to blow your brains out. You've got a copper to thank for that."

Billy didn't answer, crying instead, and he reminded George of a kid who'd been caught doing something he shouldn't, like stealing a bag of crisps from the corner shop. This was no man, not at the moment. Billy had been reduced to feeling like a child again. George knew how that felt, but he was fucked if he'd feel sorry for him. Mental health issues or not, this bloke needed taking out.

Greg had let Lillibet go and sent a message to the crew. "Where are we taking him?"

"We can't leave him at Debbie's Corner because the police and fire brigade are all over it. I know it's foggy, but someone still might see us.

Kitchen Street will be a problem for Janine when it comes to keeping Lillibet out of it. The other women might slip up when questioned that she worked there. It'll have to be Salter Road. Get our bloke there to make sure all the women stay at the top end. We'll dump him at the bottom."

Decision made, George took a phone out of Billy's pocket and switched it off one-handed. "What's the code for this?"

"There isn't one," Billy whispered.

"Is it on contract?"

"No, it's pay as you go."

"Fucking brilliant. You've done us a big favour."

It meant the police wouldn't know who owned the number and therefore wouldn't see Billy had contacted Lillibet.

George dropped the phone in his forensic hood and forced a subdued Billy downstairs and out of the house to the street behind. He punched him in the face a few times to knock him out, then stuffed him in the BMW's boot, cable tying his wrists together, but not too tight that it would leave a mark. It pissed him off having to be so careful—Jim would spot it inside a second that Billy had been tied up if the plastic chafed the skin, and how would Janine explain that away? Why would a sex worker defending herself have had cable ties to hand?

Unless she can pass it off as a sex game gone wrong.

He shut the boot quietly and climbed in the driver's seat. Greg and Lillibet sat in the back, her leaning against him, Greg's arm around her.

"Did you leave the back door unlocked for the crew?" George asked.

Greg tutted. "Fuck me, I'm not thick, bruv."

"Just checking."

George drove away, peering at Lillibet in the rearview mirror. "You all right?"

She laid a hand over her chest to hide that horrible word.

"I'll drop you at this clinic we use. They'll soon sort that. When it's healed, you can get a tattoo to cover it." God, he'd sounded so uncaring. "Sorry, I don't mean to make light of it."

"It's okay."

The carved slices weren't that deep. Was that because Billy had been hesitant in writing that word? He'd said to Peter he wanted to stop killing, so had that played a part in this?

"Tell me what happened," George said.

Lillibet stumbled over her words but got them out eventually, enough for George to know Billy was an out and out nutter who thought of sex workers as his mother yet at the same time knew they weren't. It was Janine's job to deal with that side of things, to find an explanation as to why Billy thought the way he did, but George couldn't help wondering how some killers got confused like that. He understood trauma, he'd been through it, and he had his alters, Mad and Ruffian, who took over from time to time, but not once had he, or they, got confused as to why they acted the way they did. George wanted justice, it was as simple as that. He didn't go round killing men, pretending they were his crappy fathers, Richard and Ron.

Liar. You've murdered Richard over and over again while killing men.

George grimaced. He didn't like having *anything* in common with bastards like Billy, but it seemed he did.

Fuck it.

With Lillibet safe at the clinic, cash handed over to pay for the staff's silence, Maxwell and Nate keeping guard, their dog left at her house, George drove towards Salter Road, Greg in the passenger seat.

Never so thankful that fog cloaked the East End so it would hide him killing someone out in the open, George parked behind a Kia, probably belonging to a resident, and cut the engine. The headlights snapped off, plunging them into a strange world of coiling mist, and he got out, his bearings shot to fuck.

He felt along the side of their car until he reached the boot. Greg's footsteps on the grass verge let him know his brother was on his way, and it wasn't until Greg's arm touched his that George knew for certain where he was.

"This is a blessing in one way but a pain up the arse in another," George whispered.

"The fog? Yeah, I know what you mean."

George released the boot lock, wincing at the *clunk* it made, and pushed the lid up. The interior light splashed on. He glanced around to check the fog, but it was so thick he didn't think anyone would see them. He snagged Billy's arm and sat him up. The prick was awake, muttering, sobbing, and George dug his hand in the soft-sided storage box where they kept forensic suits, cloths, and a few tools. He found a cloth and stuffed the material inside Billy's mouth, deep, so it touched the back of his throat.

Billy retched, and George chuckled.

"No fucking about laughing," Greg warned. "We need to get him sorted and piss off sharpish. I picked his knife up and brought it with us."

Together, synchronised even with limited sight, George and Greg dragged Billy out of the boot and laid him on the verge. George went back and closed the lid. They both crouched either side of Billy, and George switched his phone torch on. He was able to see better this low down, the fog loitering about a foot off the ground, the torch beam not penetrating far but giving enough light for them to work.

Greg took the decision out of George's hands on who'd make the killer blow. He sat on Billy's stomach, and George imagined a woman doing this after she and Billy had rolled around to get the upper hand after he'd tried to abduct her. Greg stabbed the blade into the side of Billy's neck. Billy jolted, his muffled scream of pain too loud for George's liking, so he slapped a gloved hand over his mouth, enough to keep him quiet but not enough to leave fingerprint bruises for Jim to find. He checked where he'd jabbed the gun into his temple, annoyed with himself at a slight bruise.

George stared Billy in the eyes. "Night-night, my old son."

Greg pulled the knife out and dropped it on the grass, like a sex worker would when she'd realised what she'd done. Blood spurted, seeping between the blades of grass and into the mud, and George directed the torch glow at it so he could see how red it was, how the loss of it was going to stop Billy's heart from beating. George imagined it splashing on his face, hot then drying cold, and wished he'd been able to slash this fucker up as much as Billy had slashed those women.

This justice felt sour, bitter--he hadn't been able to do what he'd wanted, what Billy deserved. But George conceded that sometimes—only sometimes, mind—Janine was right.

He took his own flick-knife out and sliced the cable tie, stuffing it in his suit hood, studying Billy's wrists for signs he'd been bound. As far as he could see, nothing, but that didn't mean marks wouldn't show up by the time the body was found. He switched the torch off and went back to the car. Waited for Greg to get in before he started the engine. He reversed out of the spot and down the road, doing a U-turn on the corner to leave the street the way they'd come in. Hopefully, Billy would remain undiscovered until the morning, and while George felt bad that an innocent party would find him and be traumatised by it, there was no other way they could have done it.

Janine wanted a body, and she'd get it.

Chapter Twenty-Eight

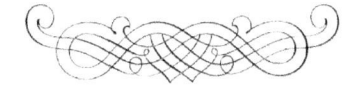

Rolanda Carroway dashed out of her house and down the garden path at half past six in the morning, still sleepy, but the slap from the cold winter air soon perked her up. She had to get to King's Cross station in time to catch the train to Edinburgh Waverley. Her niece, at university, had invited her up to see her lodgings, and Rolanda had a few gifts she wanted to give to her.

Struggling with a small suitcase in one hand and a bulging bag of presents in the other, she managed to hook her foot around her ajar gate and walk out onto the pavement. Head down, and glad the fog had gone, she lifted her arm to shift the bag handles up it so her hand was free to fish in her handbag for her car keys. She took them out and raised her head, moving towards her car, only to stop short at the sight of someone on the grass verge, the light of a lamppost illuminating him.

A man.

Was he asleep?

Sick and tired of blokes prowling this street because of the sex workers, she contemplated what to do. Go past him and squeeze between the front of her car and the back bumper of another and get into her Kia? Drive away and leave him to it? But what if he'd been there all night? He'd be so cold, and if he'd been drunk when he'd lain down, he wouldn't even know where he was when he woke.

Also sick of her conscience telling her to do the right thing—*For God's sake!*—she hurried to her boot, put her things inside, and returned to the man. She recoiled in shock, her mouth going dry. Dried blood coated his neck, and a wound about an inch long had her stumbling backwards to get away from him. Heart thudding, she let out a scream, the heel of her stiletto sinking into the ground, stalling her so quickly she plunked to the grass on her arse.

She fumbled in her handbag in search of her phone, her fingers shaking so much she couldn't put in the unlock code. Barbara from next door must have heard her screech as she came thundering down her garden path, her dressing gown fronts flapping, the waist cord swaying.

"Are you all right?" Barbara approached, a hand out to help Rolanda up.

"That man…that man…"

Barbara looked his way. "Oh fuck."

Chapter Twenty-Nine

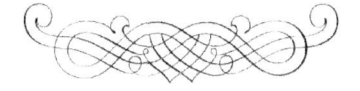

While Janine waited for the tent to be erected—and it needed to be quick as several residents had emerged from their homes to see what all the fuss was about—she sat with Rolanda Carroway in the woman's kitchen. She'd made tea, Colin pleased about that as he hadn't had a chance to drink a coffee because of the early callout. Rolanda, her neighbour beside her, cried quietly.

Janine sat opposite them and asked Rolanda and Barbara to go through what had happened earlier. It was the usual for people stumbling across a body, the confusion upon first seeing it, then the shock at the sight of blood, and the inevitable scream that had brought Barbara running.

Janine needed to know if they'd picked up on anything else—she had to arm herself with information to steer her colleagues away from it being George and Greg. "Let's rewind to last night. What did you do?"

Rolanda blinked. "What do you mean? What has that got to do with this?"

"Talk me through your evening. I'm trying to establish whether you heard anything going on out the front."

"The murder, you mean." Barbara nodded knowingly.

Janine smiled at her. She had the roundabout time Billy had been killed as she'd received a text from the twins, but she had to make sure, despite the fog, that no one had seen them. George had assured her they hadn't, but they couldn't be complacent. She dreaded the fact that one day, those two might be apprehended, and there'd be nothing she could do about it. She was amazed they'd never been caught for anything so far.

"Yes," she said. "And perhaps the sounds of someone fighting off an attacker."

Barbara shook her head. "I went to bed about eight to watch the telly. Fell asleep around ten when the news came on and didn't wake up until six. I was making a cuppa when I heard Rolanda scream."

"What about you?" Janine asked Rolanda.

"I was packing until late."

"Packing?"

"Oh God, I need to let Summer know I won't be at the train station. She's meeting me in Edinburgh." She must have seen Janine's raised-eyebrow, silent question. "My niece. I was going to stay with her for a few days. She's at university."

"Okay. So you were packing and ?"

"After that, I wrapped her presents. I got her a few bits and bobs. Anyway, I went to bed, and the last time I looked at the clock it was twelve-thirteen. I went to sleep pretty quickly and didn't hear anything going on."

Good. "Okay, a PC will come to take both of your statements. We'd best get on. Sorry you had such a shock."

"Is he one of those men, d'you know?" Rolanda asked.

Again, Janine lifted her eyebrows.

The woman blushed. "The perverts who are always down here."

"Perverts?" Janine pretended not to know what she was talking about.

Rolanda held her head in her hands and sighed. "I'm so tired of them. I can't even sell up and move because no one wants to live down here, given what goes on."

"Can you explain, please?" Janine asked, even though she knew exactly what Rolanda meant.

Barbara hefted her boobs up with her forearms. "Prostitutes."

"You mean sex workers," Janine corrected.

"Yes, they stand outside," Barbara said. "Dressed like it's summer with their legs and tits on show. They'll catch their death of cold. It's disgusting, I tell you. Kids live down here, and they shouldn't be seeing that, women getting into cars and whatnot. Some of them even give blow jobs in full view of our windows. There's got to be a law against that, surely. I bet that bloke out there got a bit too fresh with one of them and they stabbed him. Can't say I blame them if they carry a knife around with them, but at the same time, if they know their job's dangerous, why do it?"

"To feed their families like any other person on the planet," Janine snapped. She shouldn't let her personal opinions cloud an interview, but fucking hell, the ladies out there were only doing their best. "I'll leave you be."

She stalked out, past a gawping Colin who followed her to the road where they took protective clothing from the back of the SOCO van and togged up.

"What's got your goat?" he said. "Bit snippy there, weren't you?"

"Now I've got to know some of them, it pisses me off the way sex workers are viewed. Yes, I get that residents don't want them in their streets, but… Never mind. Let's go and see if the dead man has any ID on him." She tromped into the tent.

Jim crouched by the body, and Sheila stood watching while the photographer, Clive today, clicked away at his camera. Janine got her first proper glimpse of Billy Ford. He was your average man in his jeans and shirt. The latter had speckles, drips, and patches of blood on it, and it had soaked through the collar and shoulder on one side. A single knife wound to the neck, as George had told her, the knife itself lying on the grass by Billy's head. Bruising to the face where George had punched him, plus one at the temple which she could have brained him for, and scratches from Lillibet scraping her nails down his cheeks.

She might have left DNA behind. Bollocks.

Janine would prefer no evidence remained whatsoever that Billy had been with Lillibet, but she doubted that would be the case. George mentioned Billy had managed to carve LYING on her chest before they'd stopped him, and there had been blood at the house, which the crew would have visually removed, although it was unlikely they'd get rid of all of it. Forensics would find it. Her blood would have undoubtedly got onto Billy's shirt, would still be on that knife, and Janine cursed the fact that shirt hadn't been removed after he'd died. She'd be praying for an 'attacked sex worker' theme to be agreed upon, so it wouldn't have been a stretch that her punter had taken his shirt off, in the car, say, when they were about to have sex, then things had turned nasty.

Too late to do anything about it now.

Section sixty-two of PACE, the Police and Criminal Act, came to mind, or words to that effect. An officer may authorise collection of DNA if they have reasonable grounds to believe the sample will prove or disprove an individual's involvement.

Lillibet needs to keep her nose clean for the rest of her life so she isn't arrested and her DNA is kept on file and matched to this shitshow.

"Any speculation so far, Jim?" She was asking so everyone came to the conclusion she wanted them to—so *she* wasn't the one to put the idea in their heads that a sex worker had defended herself. Too many times in the past she'd put her view forward, and she worried it would be picked up if she kept doing it.

"Considering where the murder took place—or should that be manslaughter because it may well be self-defence—I'd say this was a customer getting too rough with a sex worker and she fought him off, wouldn't you?"

Janine nodded. "Could he be the Slasher?"

Jim pondered. "The knife might yield some proof of that if he used it on the other victims. Dried blood could be on that handle."

"If it *is* that scenario," Sheila said, "I'm glad the woman got away from him. It could have turned out so differently."

"Hmm." Janine told them her findings from last night, making out she felt Peter Ford had stayed on the straight and narrow since Emma Meyers had been killed—she passed on her suspicions about Rod Clarke killing Emma but that she had no proof.

"What?" Colin said. "You didn't say anything about this on the way here."

Janine stared at him across the body. "One, neither of us had even a sniff of coffee when the call came in, and two, you were in a bad mood because we had to get up early. I thought it best to leave you alone."

"I was only dogged off because the missus had a grump on when the phone woke her up. So you went round to this Peter's house, you said. Why didn't you call me in to go with you?"

"Considering what you just said about your wife, do you think that would have been a good idea? Really? Brown went with me instead."

"Right." Colin folded him arms. For someone who didn't like pulling his weight at work anymore, he was doing a bloody good job of acting like he wanted to—or showing his jealousy that a PC had accompanied her.

Janine swivelled her attention away from him. "What's your take on this, Sheila?"

"Minimal disruption at the scene. The grass hasn't been flattened down much by shoes, as you would expect if an altercation or fight had taken place here. Think about it: people would dig their feet into the ground to get better purchase if they're scrapping, and there *was* likely a fight, going by that bruise on his face."

Shit. I can't have her putting it in a report that there wasn't at least a scuffle. "They might have fought in a vehicle."

"True." Sheila sighed. "That would explain things, I suppose. But it *doesn't* explain the slight chafing on his wrists or what looks like the mark from the butt of a gun being pressed to his temple."

For fuck's sake, George… "Could have been handcuffs—you know, used in sex play. As for the bruise, maybe the sex worker had a gun for protection."

"Why not use it, then?" Sheila asked. "Because you can bet your arse that if I had a gun in my hand and had pressed it to his head, and I was scared out of my mind, I'd pull the bloody trigger, I wouldn't use a knife on him instead."

"What if he overpowered her and the gun moved away from his head?" Janine suggested. "What if, as well as being scared of him, she was also frightened of shooting him, of being accused of murder using a gun she might not have a license for? He could have dropped the knife and she picked it up."

"And she *wasn't* scared to stab him?" Sheila didn't look convinced.

"Perhaps by that point it was a case of her or him—he was going to kill her if she didn't stop him, so she had no choice."

Colin grunted. "Whatever, if he's the Slasher, then good on her, I say. Maybe his car is here and we can check inside it for evidence, unless she drove it away afterwards or he arrived on foot."

"PCs are taking down all the reg numbers now," Janine said. "We'll soon know if one doesn't belong to the residents. So, to conclude, it looks like a fatal stab to the neck, perhaps administered by a sex worker."

Murmurs of agreement went round.

Right, glad that's been established.

Clive stopped taking pictures. "Okay, I'm done until you move him. For what it's worth, I agree with you. Going by my experience of photographing thousands of scenes, this was someone killing because they had to. If you think about the panic you'd feel afterwards, you'd just run if you hadn't planned it, wouldn't you. If it was premeditated, he wouldn't be here unless the body was left for a purpose, as in, to make some kind of point or he's got something to do with the residents."

Janine could have kissed him. "Good point. She killed then ran, shitting herself. Can you check for ID, Jim?"

He put a gloved hand in Billy's jeans pocket and brought out a little wooden soldier, the trousers painted blue, the jacket red. "Err, not something I expected to find."

What the hell did Billy have that for?

"Pop this in an evidence bag, will you, Sheila?"

She took it off him.

Jim dipped into the pocket again and found a brown leather wallet. He opened it and pulled a credit card from one of the slots. "A Mr B Ford."

"Oh," Sheila said. "Not Peter, like you thought."

Janine affected shock. "Bloody hell, this puts a whole new slant on it. His son's called Billy. We'd better go." She rushed out of the tent, stripped out of her protectives on the other side of the cordon, and got in her car.

Colin joined her a minute or so later. "I thought we were going up the other end to speak to the sex workers after we'd spoken to Jim."

"We were, but the next of kin is more important, especially as I already had my suspicions regarding Peter Ford. Send the scene sergeant a message and get him to put PCs on questioning the women. Not that I imagine many are out at this time of the morning."

"Who's the scene sergeant?"

Frustrated at Colin's lack of attention, she barked, "Didn't you *see* her when we got here? Martha Phillips."

Janine drove away, heading for Peter's house. How should she play this? With the possibility that the knife would be evidence enough that Billy was the Slasher, if he'd used the same one on the victims, the only thing she could pin on

Peter was the death of Emma Meyers, but she had no proof he'd been involved.

Maybe a visit from her would rattle his cage enough to set the bird chirping.

Chapter Thirty

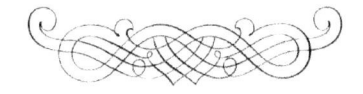

Peter had phoned Billy several times after those two men had come back to search his house last night. The cheek of them, barging in and nosing around, as if he'd lied to them that Billy wasn't there and had staged that phone call. They'd eventually left with another warning: *"Remember, not a word about this, fuckface, else you know what'll happen."*

Billy hadn't picked up any of the calls, and Peter hadn't bothered messaging him. He didn't want the police asking him questions about the content if those twins were going to kill his son—coppers would come here to talk to him. It still meant he had to explain why he'd tried to get in contact with Billy so many times, but maybe he could say he'd been worried about him after he'd spoken to him earlier that night. But then that might go against what The Brothers had told him to do. But what else was he *supposed* to do? Unless they killed Billy and buried him somewhere, so no coppers would even come knocking.

He'd sat and probed deep into his psyche about allowing the twins to kill Billy. Well, allowing wasn't the word, he didn't have a say in it. What kind of man did that make him? A bad one, a selfish one, and to save himself from admitting that without Billy around, all of this would go away, conveniently swept under the carpet, he'd given Michaela a ring to check she was okay.

It would have been eight or so where she was, and she'd just been getting ready to go down and watch the entertainment on offer at the hotel. He'd kept relatively calm, used to masking his true feelings, and didn't think she'd picked up on how worried he was. If she had, he'd have lied and said his concern was for Billy, given that they hadn't heard much from him lately. He couldn't tell her—ever—that he was shitting bricks about finally being caught for arranging Emma's murder.

He finished his third coffee at the breakfast bar, along with a small helping of cornflakes (the only thing he could stomach foodwise), and got up to pour another brew from the carafe. He was supposed to be playing golf today, but his friend had messaged around eleven last night to call it off because of the fog. That had gone now, and it left him at a bit of a loose end, an empty day stretching ahead. He couldn't stand to be by himself, his thoughts would overtake him if he did that, so maybe he'd go into the office. Darren wouldn't think he'd come to check on him, he was used to his dad dropping by for a natter, and Peter could claim he was bored without Michaela around.

Yes, he'd do that.

The doorbell rang, reminding him of last night, DI Sheldon and that PC, then The Brothers disturbing his evening twice. He recalled he had a parcel coming from Amazon, a nice bottle of Michaela's favourite perfume so, shaking off the sudden nerves that had surfaced, he went to collect it.

Sheldon and a tubby man stood on the top step.

Oh, fucking hell. Shit. Has Billy's body been found?

He raised his eyebrows. "Oh, I thought you were a delivery driver." He gave a little laugh.

"We need to come in," Sheldon said.

It was about Billy, wasn't it. It had to be.

"Can I ask why? I thought we'd established things last night." He went to fold his arms then thought better of it. This wasn't a business deal where he had to come across as uptight or confident, he had to be submissive if they were here to tell him what he thought.

"If we could just step inside, sir," the man said.

"And you are?" Peter smiled to remove the sting of his words—he hadn't meant to sound so abrupt.

"DS Colin Broadly."

"Ah, right. Okay then, well, I suppose we could have another chat to confirm things, but I really don't think it's necessary. I have a pot of coffee on, would you like one?"

"That would be lovely," Sheldon said.

He led the way into the kitchen, his nerves spiking again. Giving himself an internal talking-to so his hands didn't shake, he took two cups out of a cupboard and poured coffee. Placed their filled cups on the breakfast bar along with a little jug of cream and the bowl of sugar cubes Michaela insisted made them look a cut above. Personally, he wasn't fond of them, they didn't dissolve as quickly as he liked, but he'd never said anything. He'd learned not to let the small stuff bother him.

He sat and gestured for them to sit on the other stools. Broadly did, dragging a cup towards him, but Sheldon remained standing.

"Sorry to have come back," she said, "but I'm afraid we have some bad news."

It's Billy, it's Billy, it's Billy…

"Oh?" Peter cocked his head.

"We have reason to believe, due to the ID found, that your son, Billy, has been murdered."

"Good grief! What?"

"Your son," she said. "He was found in Salter Road on a grass verge. He'd been stabbed."

"What on *earth* was he doing *there*? He lives nowhere near it. Was his car there? He drives a Merc."

"Not that we saw."

"Bloody hell. Well, I don't know what to say."

"Probably the shock, sir. Do you know of anyone who'd want to harm him?"

Peter shook his head, thinking of how Michaela would take this. What if she had another stroke? And Darren, despite Billy whining that he was the favourite, loved his brother. This was going to devastate them.

Yet you knew it was going to happen.

Having an inkling and thinking the body would be buried was completely different to him being dumped on a bloody grass verge! How was Peter supposed to act? He racked his brain, thinking of all the true-crime programmes he'd watched where the police came with such news, and he staggered to a stool and plonked down on it.

Head in his hands, he fake sobbed, although real tears came quickly—of relief to have Billy out of his hair, to have the police focused on his son rather than him, and for the boy he'd wished Billy was when he'd first clapped eyes on him.

"My God…"

"Take a minute to process it," Sheldon said.

Peter lifted his head and stared at the wall behind her. She picked up a cup and sipped, likely used to delivering this sort of news. How did it affect her? Badly? Or was she so used to it that it failed to make a dent in her emotions?

"You said he was stabbed." He sniffed. Wiped his eyes. "May I ask where?"

"In the neck. He has bruises on his face and temple and chafe marks on his wrists."

"So he was tied up?"

Sheldon flinched. "Um, no, we believe, owing to the location, that he may have visited a sex worker. Perhaps handcuffs were used. Salter Road is a known soliciting area."

"A sex worker?" Peter barked out a hefty laugh. "He wouldn't use those. His mother was one, and he detested her for it. That's the last place he'd be."

"Maybe that's *why* he was there," Sheldon suggested. "To exorcise some demons?"

"What do you mean?"

"The knife we assume killed him was left at the scene. It will be tested to see if there's any DNA on it from the Slasher victims. We can't discount that, given that four sex workers have been killed recently. As I said, he was in a known area…"

"What?" Peter stood, hoping he appeared distraught and confused. "*What*?"

"I know this must be difficult to accept, but that's where we're at. Unless he'd have another reason for being in Salter Road?"

"He might have a friend who lives there." Untrue, Billy didn't *have* friends.

"Maybe. If he does, that will become clear when the officers have finished house-to-house enquiries. But if no one knows him…"

"Good Lord." Peter sat again, his mind racing. "If it's him… I know he was a child, but what if *he* killed Emma? What if Zeller had it wrong all along and Billy was the one he should have been looking at?"

"That would depend on Billy's size and strength at the time. Yes, a child could have done what happened to Emma, but that doesn't explain how he'd have kept her still and compliant while slicing those words into her and carving that snake. Those are the things I mentioned that also featured in the recent murders."

"Then it *must* have been him. He knew about those things because he *saw* them. He was a strong boy. Maybe Emma took a sleeping pill and he did it while she was out of it."

"There were no substances found by toxicology."

Peter was desperate to pin Emma's death on his son, but if he kept on, Sheldon would think he was overegging it. If only he'd convinced Billy to say Emma had molested him as a child, the tickling thing. Emma wouldn't have had to die then, she'd have been put in prison, and Billy wouldn't have seen her murder. He wouldn't have had his brain ruined. And this wouldn't be happening now.

"Maybe he became the Slasher because he witnessed what happened to Emma," he suggested.

"That could be likely, but it still doesn't explain who killed *her*."

"There was a man, he came to Emma's house every night for weeks. People saw him. He spoke to Billy through the letterbox."

"I'm aware of that."

"God, this messed him up more than we thought."

"What do you mean by that?"

Peter sighed. "I never wanted to admit this to anyone, but I suppose I'll have to now. Billy was...difficult. We covered up for him, made excuses. We told ourselves that the trauma had changed him, that he couldn't help being strange, but we came to the conclusion, once he was a teen, that it was more than that. His therapist might be able to help you. Perhaps she can release his files now he's...he's dead." He choked out a sob. "Sorry, I'll be all right in a second, it's just...it's just a lot to take in."

"I understand." Sheldon waited for a moment, then prompted, "What was he really like, then?"

"Oh, I don't know how to explain it. Odd. Like he'd look at us funny sometimes, and he wasn't fond of Michaela playing the mother role. He resented her for being alive when Emma wasn't, I'm sure of it." He prepared his lie. "He told me once that sex workers were dirty animals and needed to be 'eradicated', that was the word he used. I didn't think anything of it, didn't think he'd *do* anything about it, but... Then there was the trouble he liked to cause. Getting his brother blamed for things he'd done. Stupid things, like stealing money from my wallet or breaking the kitchen window. Generally being a pest."

"Can you shed any light on why he'd have a toy soldier in his pocket?"

Peter shuddered. "Mr Spencer, that's what he called him. He talked to him, and a few years after he moved in with us, he responded in a different voice, as if the soldier was chatting to him. This is what I meant by him being odd. The therapist said he'd latched on to the toy as you would a safety blanket, that he'd held it while his mother was being killed and he'd felt safer knowing the soldier was there. Any time he did something he'd get into trouble with us for, he squeezed the soldier. I felt sorry for him, of course I did, but all the same, it was weird."

"Thanks for that. When was the last time you spoke to Billy?"

Oh God. What should I say?

They'd go through his phone and know, so he had to go with the truth. If The Brothers came back, he'd explain.

"Last night, actually. I rang him to ask if he wanted to come over to watch a film. Now I'm thinking about it, he was odd then, too."

"In what way?"

"He was whispering, and when I asked why, he said he was hiding from someone."

"Who?"

"I don't know."

"Did he say anything else?"

"No."

She stared at him as if she knew he was lying, but how could she? The twins wouldn't have told her what had been said. She was a copper, for God's sake!

"I phoned him several times after that, concerned about him, but he didn't answer."

Sheldon nodded to herself. "Last time we were here you said your wife was away. Is there anyone else who can come and sit with you? You've had a shock so…"

"Darren, my son."

"We could do with speaking to him, too."

Peter almost shouted *no*, because Darren didn't need to be dragged into this, but there was no choice. "Okay. I'll phone him now."

Sheldon didn't budge, there was no privacy to be had, so Peter had to speak to his son with her beady eye on him—leaving the room would appear suspicious. He gave the news as gently as he could, then told Darren to get a taxi over as driving after that sort of shock wasn't a good idea. He'd sounded caring, hadn't he?

An hour later, Sheldon seemingly happy with the information she'd gleaned from Darren, who'd surprisingly been open with his feelings about Billy by saying he'd always known something was off about him but he'd felt sorry for him, Peter breathed out a sigh of relief.

"I'll look into Emma's case again," Sheldon said. "I'll have to, as it's clear her death affected Billy if he does turn out to be the Slasher."

Peter nodded. "Do what you have to."

She stared him in the eye. "Clarke would have done the same."

Peter's knee-jerk reaction was to ask her what the fuck she'd meant by that, but he nodded, scared out of his mind. "He would."

"And Zeller."

What was she getting at?

"I'll get to the bottom of who killed Emma," she said. "Finally put it to bed."

He felt his face drain, wished he had control of that so she couldn't see how her words had put the fear of God into him, but he didn't, and his body had betrayed him.

"We'll see ourselves out."

She gave him a horrible look, one that chilled him to the bone. She knew. She fucking *knew*. Then she and Broadly walked out, leaving him alone with his second-born son, a thousand questions parading through his mind.

"Mum," Darren said. "This could finish her off."

Peter nodded. He had to focus on his wife and remaining child now and hope Sheldon dug deep but found nothing except the ashes of Emma's investigation, nothing that would reignite and point the finger at him. "We'll leave it until she's home."

"But what if it hits the news? You know how she reads the papers on her phone."

Again, Peter silently cursed Billy. Yet one more thing he had to deal with when it came to that bloody boy.

Fucking bastard kid.

Chapter Thirty-One

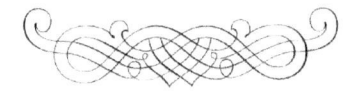

Lillibet couldn't pack her stuff fast enough. She needed to get the hell out of here now Billy's body had been found. Thank God she had help. Debbie, still at a loose end without Moon, joined in with folding clothes and putting them into suitcases, but the twins had sent some men round to do all the rest. It had been horrible just now in the living room, seeing a bloke wrapping her ornaments in newspaper with a Slasher headline on the front page, and Debbie had snapped at him to ditch that sheet and use one without the killer's story on it.

Lillibet's chest itched. Billy hadn't gone deep, he'd lightly scored the word LYING, but it was visible enough that she'd see it every day while there were still scabs. The nurse at the clinic had said it wouldn't scar much, if at all, which was something, but maybe she'd do as George had said and get a tattoo right across her chest anyway. Flowers or something pretty.

George and Greg had found her a place to live, and she'd have a friend there. Lillibet was going up north, moving into a house next door to Pippa on the Barrington Patch. She'd be working for a man called Jimmy, which would always create a link in her mind to the Jimmy Riddle here, and Jim the pathologist Janine had mentioned, although the northern one was much younger. She'd be working doing what she'd done at Fords', except it would be to invest money for Cassie Grafton and the gangland business Jimmy ran for her. It was an exciting but daunting thing to be doing, but in her mind she had no choice. The need to run away trumped everything else.

Her phone rang, Janine's burner number on the screen.

Debbie clocked it. "Answer her. It might be something you need to know before you leave."

Lillibet swiped. "Hello?"

"I've got to be quick. I'm in the thick of things here and have only just got a minute to speak to you. I'm at Billy's house. Forensics have discovered blood on the floor despite the carpet being removed by the crew and the stains being bleached—there was never any doubt that would happen, I expected it. But it'll be matched to blood on Billy's shirt—there's no way it didn't get on there, even a small speck will be enough. There's nothing I can do to stop that happening. Listen to me, and remember what I say. Take cash wages up north so you can deny any involvement with Grafton's people should they ever get nicked and you get dragged into it. Fuck the taxman, that isn't important in the grand scheme of things."

"Okay."

"Personally, I think it's mad you're going to be working for them, you're putting yourself in the firing line with having a DNA sample taken by the police if you get caught as a member of their firm, but as you're sure what you want to do, all I'll say is this: If you ever get arrested, and your sample is taken and matched to this mess, you claim self-defence and that you ran through fear, got it? I'll make sure you only get a rap on the knuckles as best I can, but I can't promise anything. Just…just keep below the radar, all right?"

Lillibet thought about Pippa and what she was getting up to. "What about Pippa? She's going around *hurting* people for Jimmy, and I'll be living next door to her."

"For fuck's sake! What was George thinking?"

"I don't know, I'm just doing what he said and packing. There's a van outside waiting to take everything up there. Debbie's driving me."

"Then you're going to have to be a bitch if the shit hits the fan and make out you don't know Pippa. Yes, it'll come out in any investigation that you worked on Kitchen with her, but you weren't good mates, understand, and you were surprised when you moved away to find she lived there, too. God, that's not going to sound plausible. Um…"

Lillibet imagined Janine tapping her foot, trying to find a solution.

"Sod it, we'll deal with it if it comes to that. Just don't get caught up too much with that lot where you lose sight of why you're going there. This, what's happening here, must always be at the front of your mind when it comes to saving your arse. I've got to go. Good luck."

The call ended, and Lillibet tossed the phone in her handbag. She told Debbie what had been said. "Am I making a mistake by running?"

Debbie sat on the bed. "I think you're panicking and want to distance yourself, yes. Janine will sort everything, and I doubt very much you'd ever get nicked here so long as you gave up sex work and did whatever it was you did at Fords', but with a different company. I understand wanting to run away, believe me, I did it, and it turned out to be the best thing I've ever done, so I can't really give advice."

"So I should still go?"

"What's your heart saying?"

"To leave."

"And your head?"

"Definitely leave."

Debbie shrugged. "Then go, but watch yourself. You can always use Barrington as a stopgap. Get all this settled in your mind then fuck off somewhere else after a few months. Come on, let's get the rest of these clothes packed. I can stay up there with you for a bit if you like, check the area out, see who this Jimmy really is and tell him you can't be compromised. Moon's not going to be back for a couple of months—don't ask, I'm a bit pissed off he'll be gone for so long—and Lisa runs The Angel anyway. The corner takes care of itself, and I have Amaryllis and Belladonna who sort the parlour, so it's not like I need to be here all the time."

Lillibet nodded. "All right."

Debbie's mobile rang. She glanced at the screen and answered it on speaker. "I'm with Lillibet, and she can hear you. What's up?"

"We've just been through Billy's phone," George said. "The fucker had cameras on lampposts on Kitchen and your corner. We've found them and got rid, but that's how he knew what the women were doing while they were at work. It could also be on his laptop, and the police will see it."

Lillibet gasped. "That's why we felt like we were being watched."

Debbie nodded. "Okay, thanks for giving us that creepy information, George."

"You're welcome. Oh, and he had the tinkling of wind chimes saved. No idea what that was about."

"Me neither. Maybe that's something Janine needs to know."

"I'll ring her now. Tarra."

Debbie popped her phone in her bag. "What a bloody weirdo. Billy, not George."

Lillibet folded a pair of jeans, her eyes brimming. She'd made something of herself here before Billy had wrecked it. Debbie had paid her well, and she had no debts anymore. She loved working with the women on Kitchen, but life as a sex worker was closed to her now. She'd never put herself in such a dangerous position again.

She let the tears fall for a while, then switched her mind to new horizons. She wasn't doing anything illegal up north except crunching numbers and sorting investments, it was just her new bosses were dodgy, that was all.

It would be all right. It had to be. There was no way she was going down for killing the Slasher when George and Greg were the ones to blame.

Chapter Thirty-Two

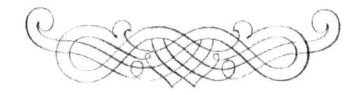

One month later – December 24th

Janine finally had a lead. She'd persuaded the DCI to let her do a television appeal, asking for the public's help in Emma Meyers' murder. He'd argued that it was a cold case, and she'd fired back that it was linked to the Slasher and he couldn't dispute that.

"How can you *not* let me do this?" she'd raged. "The wording on the chests, the snake, Zeller confirmed it. We might well have proof from the knife that Billy killed those four women, but someone else killed his mother, and I'm telling you, it was Clarke."

"Jesus Christ, Janine. Can you imagine the backlash if it *was* him? A bloody *copper* killing a sex worker?"

"Let's not forget I've got him down for killing Annabel Hawkins an' all. The files had been tampered with using her name, I told you this. She said it wasn't her. Who else could it have been but Clarke? And, with all due respect, who gives a *fuck* what the public think about a copper being involved? I want justice for Emma, and I'm going to bloody get it."

He'd relented.

Someone had come forward, and she was meeting him now. Alone. She didn't want Colin in on this, nor had she entertained taking a bobby with her. Spooking the bloke with two officers wasn't anything she'd contemplate. She had an agreement with the twins to let them have a go at Peter in the warehouse, but like with Billy, she wanted a body. And a written confession. And no bruises this time.

She stood outside The Golden Lion in the West End, the street bustling with people doing a bit of last-minute Christmas shopping. The pub, sandwiched between a department store and a Superdrug, had people standing outside smoking ciggies and vapes. Fairy lights twinkled in all the shop windows, a few Christmas trees standing front and centre behind the glass, the baubles a myriad of sparkling colours.

Everyone had bundled up in thick coats, scarves, and hats, their breath puffing out as if they smoked like the pub patrons. The perfect scene, except Janine didn't belong in it. She wished she did, that she could be at home now with Cameron, drinking eggnog or something equally as festive, but alcohol wasn't on her menu as she was on duty. Instead, Cameron stood against the pub wall and would follow her inside as though he was a customer, and she had a job to do. No time to join the Christmas Eve fun—or aggravation, going by the face of one woman who breezed past with her friend, muttering about the supermarket being all out of cranberry sauce and that her Simon would be grumpy about it.

Janine took a deep breath and pushed the pub door open. The witness had said he'd have a red scarf on so she'd be able to spot him, and she'd agreed to do the same; she'd had to buy hers earlier as she didn't own one that colour.

He sat in the far-right corner, around sixty or so, hair greying in patches. He appeared well-to-do, distinguished, and reminded her a little of Zeller, who'd no doubt be pleased Emma's killer would be revealed in the forced confession the twins would get later, although she'd bet it wouldn't be who he'd thought.

She checked Cameron walked in behind her, held a finger up to the witness that she was just getting a drink, and approached the bar. She ordered a Diet Coke for herself and a Guinness for the man—his current pint sat on the table in front of him, half gone. She paid and walked over, placing his glass down as she sat opposite him.

"DI Janine Sheldon," she said.

"Locky Henshaw." He didn't *sound* well-to-do, his accent pure East End, but not as rough as George's and Greg's, as if he'd lived in the West End for a while which had shaved off the harsh edges.

"Unusual name."

"It's not my real one. I run a locksmith business."

She drank some Coke. "Are you prepared to give me your proper name?"

"Yep, although you might laugh."

"I could do with a bit of levity. Go on."

"Ptolemy." He'd said it with a silent P.

"Um, what's so funny? Sounds nice enough to me."

"It's after Claudius Ptolemy, an astronomer, mathematician, and geographer. My old mum liked history. The funny bit is, I'm none of those things." He shrugged. "Maybe it's one of those jokes that's only amusing in the family. My brother's called Darwin, poor sod."

She smiled. "Okay, so what did you see and hear? Sorry to switch subjects, but as you can imagine, I need to catch whoever did this. Can I ask—and again, I apologise for firing questions at you—why didn't you come forward when it happened?"

"To be honest, I didn't think it was anything to tell until the appeal went out earlier."

She frowned. "So you didn't realise that the conversation was about Emma Meyers? I mean, surely you'd heard about in on the news when she died."

"Let me start at the beginning—we're jumping all over the shop here. The night I heard them, I was off on holiday in the early hours. Me and the wife went for a month-long cruise, so I didn't hear about Emma until we got back, and by then, it was kind of old news, plus I was focused on work more than anything, driven, so didn't pay it any mind."

"Right…"

"I came here with Sarah, that's the missus, after we'd done our packing. We had a bit of dinner, then a drink or two after. I sat there." He pointed to the table beside them. "And they sat here. Two men. I recognised one of them, Peter Ford."

Got you, you smug bastard.

"He was just becoming prominent, had featured in the local rag for his charity donations. I remember it was definitely him because I was an envious prick back then and wished I'd gone into the investment and banking world instead of being a locksmith. Mind you, since then I've built my business up to be countrywide, so I'd say I'm raking it in as much as him."

Janine sighed inwardly at him going off topic. "What about the other man?"

"Peter called him Clarke. Does that mean anything to you?"

Janine's insides seemed to scramble. "Yes, it does." *I fucking* knew *it was him*.

"What did you overhear?"

"Peter rambled on about some woman; he was angry. They kept saying *her* instead of a name, and if I'd heard her name, then I'd definitely have cottoned on when I read about Emma in the paper. To me she was just an unknown woman, know what I mean? Anyway, Peter said she hadn't done a test to prove her son was his and he'd had enough of her leaving the boy on his own while she went to work. In a jokey way, he said Clarke ought to kill her for him."

"And you didn't think that was cause for concern?"

"No, because of how it was said and how it panned out next. Clarke laughed and told him to fuck off, he wanted nothing to do with it, then Peter mentioned he'd pay him. Said hypothetically he'd give him cash every so often until he'd paid him off, said he drew money out for his wife enough times that a couple of hundred more wouldn't be noticed. Clarke shook his head, said it was crazy, but yes, that would work because Peter's bank statements would be scrutinised for anything iffy on the money front. He reckoned Peter would be a suspect, you know, that…what was it he said? He'd be seen as an upset man who'd hired a hitman."

"And this still didn't make you think anything of it?" *Is he for real?*

"Now bear in mind that all this came off as theoretical. They sounded like they were imagining it but wouldn't do it. Then Clarke said Peter was better off going to the courts to get a letter sent to the woman about doing the test. I whispered to Sarah that they must be three sheets to the wind if they were nattering like that, and she said to take no notice, reckoned it was like that phrase people say, 'I'm going to kill him.' They don't actually *mean* it. I've said it loads of times. Like when someone messes up at work."

Janine nodded. "I understand where you're coming from. Still, it's weird to listen to that sort of thing and not think anything much of it."

"What can I say? That's just how it was."

"Did they speak about anything else?"

"They went on about Peter's swimming pool after that, some trouble with the pump, and it was as if the other conversation wasn't important, just guff, so me and Sarah forgot about it. Then I saw the appeal for information about Emma earlier and, I don't know, maybe because I'm older and have more consideration for these things now, it struck me that Peter and Clarke might have had something to do with it after all. I feel bad for being so absorbed in my own life in the past that I didn't put the two events together. And it was *Peter*, for God's sake. Mr Perfect. Mr Charitable. Will I be in trouble for not saying anything? Will Sarah?"

"No. What you've said is plausible. But I need to check—do you know Peter, as in, *know* him? Like, when I investigate further, am I going to find any reason you might have covered up for Peter when he and Clarke discussed this?"

Locky's eyebrows shot up. "Absolutely not! I knew him from that newspaper article, and that's all."

"So you don't want to get him in the shit now because, as you yourself said, you were envious of his wealth?"

Locky sighed. "It could look that way, I'll give you that, but no, I all but shit myself when I saw the appeal today and the cogs slotted together. It twigged for Sarah, too."

"What was it, specifically, that clued you in?"

"The name Billy being mentioned in the same breath as Emma. That was what Peter and Clarke called the boy when they were talking. It wasn't in the papers when Emma died. If it had been, it would have triggered my memory then. I think it said something about him being a minor so he couldn't be named."

That sounded about right.

"So you're prepared to go on record with this? You *and* Sarah?" she asked. "Not meaning to sound rude or doubt you, but it would be more credible to have two witnesses."

"Yep, of course we are, otherwise I wouldn't be here."

"Okay, give me a minute. I need to make a call." Janine quickly swigged some Coke then gave Cameron the nod to keep an eye on Locky while she was outside—she didn't want the man bolting, despite him saying he'd give evidence. She walked past the smokers and down the street until she found an alley between shops. Burner phone out, she rang the twins.

"What's up?" George asked. "Don't you know it's Christmas?"

"Whatever you've got planned, ditch it. You have to go and get Peter Ford—*now*—before my lot show up at his door."

"Shit. What's gone on?"

"A witness came forward. I've got limited time before I need to action officers to go to his address. You've got an hour, but remember, I want a confession and the body."

"Fuck me, every sodding Christmas gets ruined by something. I knew it was too good to be true. We were just about to play Cluedo with Will and Ichabod."

"I'm sure we've had this conversation before… Well, even if we have, here's what's in the envelope: George and Greg Wilkes, at Peter's house, with the revolver—which *won't* be used except for threatening." She cut the call and returned to Locky. "Did you drive here?"

"No, I walked."

"Okay, we'll finish our drinks, then I'll take you home to collect Sarah. We'll go down the station, and you can give a formal statement. I'll have to go and speak to Peter, so someone else will interview you."

"Will you tell him who grassed him up?"

"No."

"But we'll have to go to court so it's bound to come out in the end."

You won't. "Don't worry about it. You've done the right thing." She held her glass up and chinked it against his. "Cheers. You've made my day."

Chapter Thirty-Three

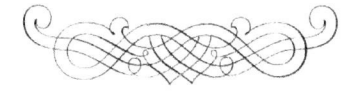

Peter lugged his suitcase to the front door. Michaela and Darren had already jetted off to Cape Verdi last week where they'd all spend Christmas. He eagerly looked forward to swimming in the Atlantic and getting a tan, enjoying the nucleus that was him, his wife, and his son, no Billy there to ruin it. He appreciated the fact they'd come through this without

Michaela having another stroke and dying from it. She'd been devastated about Billy, of course she had, but it hadn't taken the wind from her sails this time. Maybe she was secretly relieved they wouldn't have to put up with him anymore.

Peter had persuaded Darren to leave the Christmas closing of the business to him, seeing as he worked so hard all year and deserved a longer holiday. Besides, Michaela had clung to her boy ever since the news of Billy being the Slasher had come out, and Peter had felt they could do with some time alone before he joined them. This was one time he was glad Darren hadn't found a partner yet. Having one of those on the scene while they continued to process the fallout from Billy's killing spree would seem wrong. Intrusive.

He had an hour before he had to leave for the airport so went into the lounge and switched the telly on. This downtime would give him some peace, the calm before the storm of travelling at such a busy time of year. He anticipated a bustling airport, everyone in Christmas hats and tinsel scarves perhaps, the air full of the happiness generated on the night before the big day.

He'd bought Michaela an eternity ring and planned to give it to her tomorrow after she'd opened her other presents. His way of finally showing her his appreciation. So many times recently, he'd thought of what he'd put her through by using sex workers for his kinks. What an arrogant twat he'd been. That woman had remained loyal, even when he'd announced one of his extra-marital dalliances had produced a son, for goodness sake, and she'd stuck by him when others wouldn't have. She'd provided a stable home for Billy, and despite the ungrateful wanker throwing it back in her face over and over again, she'd tried her best to win him over.

Sadly, Billy had been a selfish little cunt who hadn't known which side his bread was buttered.

The funeral had been a more tragic affair than it would have been had Billy died of an illness, that awful Mr Spencer in the coffin with him. For him to have been murdered by a woman he'd planned to kill was a terrible blow to the family, not to mention shameful and embarrassing. Thank God the news hadn't tainted the business—Peter had personally visited every one of their clients to assure them that Billy's antics had been as much a shock to him and Darren as it had been to them. It would have been the final insult if Billy's behaviour had ruined Ford and Sons. Ford and *Son*, he had to remind himself, as he didn't consider Billy a relation anymore. He rued the day he'd set eyes on the little monster.

The local ten o'clock news came on, and he rose to get himself a whiskey from the sideboard. Mid-pour, he paused at the horrific words coming out of the television.

"Police have launched an appeal to the public for anyone who has information on the murder of Emma Meyers…"

His blood ran cold, and he guzzled the whiskey already in his glass.

"Police urge anyone who saw or heard anything to come forward. Detective Inspector Sheldon had this to say…"

Peter turned to the television. Sheldon stood outside a building in the dark, only her top half visible, the word POLICE behind her on a lit-up sign attached to the bricks. A yellow glow covered her, as if she was beneath a streetlamp. Microphones appeared at chest height.

"It has come to light that certain aspects of the recent murders regarding Lola Jennings, Verity Smith, Olivia Lock, and Sharny Baker are linked to another case from years ago. Emma Meyers suffered the same types of knife wounds, and we're asking for your help so we can find out who killed her. It's doubtful it was Billy Ford, her son, as he was eight years old at the time of her death, but we are intent on establishing who murdered his mother. If anyone remembers anything, however small you might think it is, please get in contact on the number at the bottom of your screen."

"Is there a possibility Billy Ford wasn't the Slasher?" someone off-camera asked.

"No, the evidence is clear regarding Billy Ford."

"Did he commit the murders because of what he saw when his mother was killed?"

"We don't know because he's dead and we can't ask him."

"So did he copy whoever killed Emma?"

"That would be supposition at this point. I'd rather deal with hard evidence."

"What about his father, Peter? DI Zeller made no bones about the fact he thought he was involved; I remember it well, I covered the story."

Peter's guts went south.

"Again, supposition. Peter Ford was cleared during the original investigation. He had an alibi."

"But alibis can be manufactured."

"That's all I'm prepared to say at this time. Thank you."

She walked away, and the shot cut to the newsreader in the studio.

"As DI Sheldon said, get in touch if you recall anything." He paused, and a mugshot appeared beside him. "A man has been arrested for indecent exposure today in what can only be described as a grooming incident…"

Peter grabbed the remote and switched the telly off. His name being mentioned… Jesus wept! Was Zeller the type to have chatted to the journalist before the appeal, getting him to say that? Sheldon hadn't committed to anything regarding Peter, which was a good thing, but what if she dug further and found something? What if someone came forward? Had he and Clarke been louder than they'd thought in The Golden Lion? Could someone have overheard their conversation about Clarke killing Emma?

He'd worried about that for years, convincing himself that if someone *had* heard, they'd surely have reported it to the police. No one had, so he'd told himself he was being paranoid.

"Shit!" He threw his glass at the wall, panic taking hold. Sheldon would come here again, he had no doubt about it, if only because that *fucking* journalist had put his name in her head.

Sod waiting, he'd go to the airport now. Piss off on holiday and deal with this when he got back. Was that the first appeal? Did he have time to leg it? Or had it gone out earlier as well? He couldn't tell, it had been dark where Sheldon stood, but that didn't mean anything because it was bloody well dark by four o'clock!

He checked his briefcase—passport, everything he needed, yes, they were in there, like they had been the last three times he'd looked—then he carried it to the front door. He'd cancel the taxi he'd arranged for eleven and drive there, use the long-stay parking and pray there was a space because he hadn't prebooked a spot. He swung the front door open and, as he was about to grab his suitcase handle, he stopped short.

Oh fuck. *Fuck*!

George, in a forensic suit, smiled at him. "Going somewhere, my old son?"

Chapter Thirty-Four

In the warehouse, George paced in front of Peter who sat on the wooden chair, fully dressed, no ropes around him. This was going to be a pain in the arse, not being able to torture him as he'd like. Janine had reamed him a new arsehole over Billy—leaving the shirt on, the bruise at the temple, shaped suspiciously like the end of a gun—and he didn't fancy having to get lairy with her if she took it upon herself to shout at him like that again.

While he had sympathy for her and what she'd been through as a teen, he didn't appreciate her getting too big for her boots. She'd been like that when they'd first approached her to take over from Clarke, but she'd learned to rein it in. Lately, more so with the Billy Ford shite, she'd become gobby. Still, he'd do what he could to prevent any argy-bargy. Personally, he thought her hormones were up the swanny or something. Maybe she'd been on her period when she'd bawled him out.

"So, here's how this is going to go." He smiled at Peter who eyed up his forensic suit. "What, you want to know why I've got this on? Isn't it obvious? I don't want anything from me, our van, or this place transferring to my clothes."

"Please don't hurt me. My wife, she won't be able to cope…"

"See, this is the thing with people like you. They don't think about anyone but themselves until it's too late. Your wife—Michaela, isn't it?— she doesn't deserve what's coming her way, neither does your Darren, and Emma didn't either. All she did was try to make a living, to bring her son up the best way she knew how, then you came back into her life and fucked everything up because you're *selfish*. That kid would have grown up better without you. Lola, Verity, Olivia, and Sharny wouldn't be *dead*. Their families wouldn't be spending their first Christmas without them. We've done some digging, found a few people from back then, and Emma was a good woman. Hannah Bishop and her daughter had a lot of nice things to say about her."

Peter blinked as if he couldn't comprehend that George and Greg had done their due diligence.

"I see you're having trouble processing that, but it's all right, I can spell it out for you. Emma may have been a troubled teenager, but she got herself sorted until she met you and got pregnant with Billy. She never told anyone other than Hannah who the father was, but she *did* tell other people you were weird, perverted, and you told her you loved her. Cruel bastard. You had no intention of leaving Michaela, did you? You strung Emma a line to keep her sweet. You used her, manipulated her emotions. Just think, if you hadn't found out she'd had a kid, life would be so different for all of you now. Billy wouldn't have been fucked up for a start—and that kind of thing naffs me off, because *I* wouldn't have been fucked up if *my* father hadn't done what he did either. But that's by the by. This isn't about me."

George walked back and forth, itching to get his cricket stump off the table behind Peter and ram it where the sun didn't shine. Greg, standing nearby, shook his head.

George held both hands up. "I wasn't going to, bruv, I swear."

Greg grimaced. "You were."

"I only thought about it for a second."

Greg crossed his arms. "Get on with it."

Peter tracked George with his eyes, his hands clasped tightly on his lap. What was he thinking? Was he working out what he could say to get out of this?

"We know, by the way." George paused and glared at him. "You and Clarke."

"Oh God…"

"That's a confession right there, but I want a full one, in writing, but we'll come to that in a minute." George glanced at the ceiling. "See that metal ring up there and that rope?"

Peter shifted his sights that way and nodded, whimpering.

Forensics would go over the rope, thoroughly checking for any shit that might be transferred, and George had been extra careful to ensure it didn't have evidence on it that would link back to them. Yes, they might find out where it was made, where it had been bought—months ago with cash by one of the twins' men in disguise—but it had been stored in plastic shrink-wrap along with all the other rope they used to tie people to the chair. It was as safe as they could get it, and the plastic sheeting on the floor was an extra layer of protection.

George flicked the rope with his gloved hand. "You're going to be dangling from that in a bit, it'll be as if you killed yourself, then we're going to take you somewhere and recreate you hanging. And you're going to have a suicide note in your pocket. Get up."

Peter obeyed, darting his gaze towards the door.

"Pointless," George said. "We'd catch you before you got anywhere near it. Go and sit at the table, you fanny."

The scumbag stumbled on his way there, and he sat in front of a single sheet of paper taken from a pad George had found at Peter's house, plus a pen and an envelope from the drawer of the sideboard in his living room. He'd popped them in a large sandwich bag for the journey here, one from Peter's kitchen drawer, and they now rested on more plastic sheeting that covered the entire table.

"You're going to admit what you got Clarke to do. Step by step, all of it, and you're going to put at the end that you're sorry. Emma's parents wanted fuck all to do with her or Billy, but I still think it's a nice touch for you to apologise to them. And your wife. And Darren. Get on with it."

Peter picked up the pen. "I… Please, don't make me do this."

George crowded him and grinned. "If you don't, I'll go after your missus and son when they get back from that little jaunt they've gone on."

Peter frowned. "How…how did you know?"

"Sheldon's one of us. She messaged me just after we got here. Cape Verdi, yes?"

"Sheldon?"

"You must be thick as pig shit if you didn't figure it out. How the *fuck* would we know to come and pick you up tonight?"

"That bitch…"

"Yeah, she can be, but it's to our advantage. Now *get writing*."

Peter wrote the first shaky word, and George left him to it, going over to Greg who watched Peter with his eyes narrowed.

"Are you in pain?" Greg smirked.

"What, because I can't ram that fucking stump up his arse? Yeah."

"This is the only way, hanging him."

"I know, but I still want to hurt him. And if Clarke were alive, I'd fuck him over good and proper for this. He *worked* for us, knowing he'd killed Emma and that copper, yet he told us he had no skeletons."

"Well, he did, we already knew that way before now, and he's gone, so there's no point winding yourself up about it."

"He'd do anything for money, the ponce."

"Even killing, but many people would. Look at all those on our payroll." Greg paused and nodded towards Peter. "We'll need to scrutinise what he's putting in case he thinks he's clever by adding some sort of code in there, dropping us in the shit."

George glanced at Peter. "You reckon he's that sneaky?"

"Yep."

George and Greg stood behind him. George scanned the words, but he couldn't see anything that would be picked up by an analyst. Peter was getting straight to the point, short and sweet, basically: *I paid Rod Clarke to kill Emma Meyers and Annabel Hawkins. This is how we did it*. He'd gone on to explain a few things, mentioning that the man who'd spoken through the letterbox had been him, not whoever Shadow Man was, and he'd coached Billy on what to say to the police and a therapist when he'd finally spoken about his mother's death.

What a complete bastard, making Billy do that.

George almost felt sorry for the lad—but not the man, never him.

"Who's Shadow Man?" George asked, in case *that* was the hidden code.

"A man who I wanted the murder blamed on. Ask Sheldon, she'll tell you."

"Right."

Peter got on with the apology to Emma's family, sounding sincere, at least on paper, but George didn't think he meant it. Until it came to saying sorry to his wife and son. Now *that*, he meant, and George reckoned the words 'I love you both with all of my heart' were genuine an' all.

Peter signed it then pushed the paper away, tossing the pen down, anger evident in that gesture. "Kill me. Just get it over with."

"You need to put the paper in the envelope and write on the front first."

"What do you want me to put on it?"

"DI Sheldon."

Peter sighed, gritted his teeth, and did as he was told.

"Now put the envelope and pen in your pocket."

Peter stood, folded the envelope, and stuffed it in the back pocket of his jeans, sliding the pen in beside it.

George smiled his predatory smile. "Over here, then."

He expected Peter to run, to at least try to get away in a last-ditch attempt to save his life, but it seemed he'd rather snuff it than face his wife and son, the press, the police, all of it. Maybe that's what happened to people who'd done something so rotten: when they got caught, they knew damn well it was all over, so what was the point in carrying on?

George looped the noose around Peter's neck. "Stand on that stool."

Another item taken from Peter's house. The only issue was Peter's car still being parked on his driveway, but Janine could smooth that over. She'd have to say he walked to the woods with the stool and rope. Whatever.

Peter climbed onto it.

George took a deep breath, quieting Mad who asked to come out and play. *Sod off, you're not allowed.* "You're going to literally crap your pants, Mr Ford, piss yourself, and whatever comes out the bottom of your jeans will be collected in a bowl which my dear brother will put beneath your feet when the stool gets kicked away. We'll sprinkle it where we take you so the scene's as close to being real as it can be."

Peter closed his eyes.

George took the end of the dangling piece of rope coming from the other side of the metal ring and wrapped it around his hand and elbow a few times, then held the length in front of him in a two-handed grip. He walked backwards, the rope tightening, pulling the noose against Peter's neck until only the toes of his shoes touched the stool. Peter automatically raised his hands to scrabble at the noose—good, it would look more authentic; despite wanting to hang themselves, people's natural response was to reach up and try to wrench the rope loose.

George paused.

Checked his watch. Just after midnight.

"Merry Christmas, sunshine." He kicked the stool away and held on.

Chapter Thirty-Five

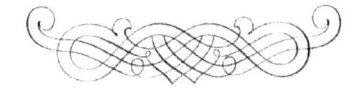

Janine couldn't help but marvel at how well the twins had played this. Peter's shoes even had debris on the soles from the ground, and the bottoms of the stool legs did, too. To her eye, this was what she'd wanted it to be—Peter killing himself.

She stood beside Colin, Jim, and Sheila in a row, all of them gazing up at the bloated face of the man who'd killed Emma, although the others didn't know that yet. Jim had already checked the pockets and found the envelope, which contained his confession. It wouldn't be opened until it had arrived at the lab, but George had assured her that everything she needed had been written.

She sighed as Jim announced Peter could be lowered, then made her way towards the poor cow who'd found the body. Natasha Sherwood had discovered it while jogging — clearly the location, Daffodil Woods, where the refugee women from another case had been buried, didn't faze her enough to go for a run elsewhere.

Janine prepared herself to go through the motions with her, then she'd take that envelope to the lab herself. She wanted to be one of the first people to see it. After that, she'd go and pop in on Zeller.

Zeller handed her a cup of tea in his kitchen, Colin grabbing his mug a bit too forcefully and spilling it on the white table.

"Bloody hell, Col," Janine muttered; God, she wanted to punch him.

"What? I'm thirsty."

Janine rolled her eyes at Zeller. "Please excuse him."

Zeller chuckled and mopped up with his jumper sleeve. "He reminds me of Clarke in that respect."

Colin's eyebrows rose. "Oi, that was a bit rude."

"I meant he was clumsy at times."

Janine sipped some tea and asked herself if she really needed to feel as smug as she did regarding what she'd come here to say. No, she shouldn't crow about it, she should deliver the news respectfully—after all, even coppers made mistakes, and she wasn't perfect by any means, especially when it came to the realisation she'd come to before she'd set out for the crime scene this morning.

She smiled. "So, we've got a tidbit for you, and it goes without saying that it can't go any further. I'm here as a courtesy because you headed Emma's case."

"It was Peter, wasn't it." Zeller folded his arms, looking as smug as Janine had felt.

"No. His body was found not long ago, though. He'd hung himself from a tree in Daffodil Woods. An envelope was in his pocket. I read the letter inside." She paused. "It was Clarke."

Zeller shot to his feet. "What?" He paced. "*That* slimy little fucker? He worked with me all through that bloody case, and I didn't suspect a thing. Fuck me sideways."

"I'd rather not," Janine said and smiled.

Zeller grinned back. "Thanks for trying to make me feel better, but... I had no idea. What happened? How did it even come about?"

Janine explained what Locky had told her, then sipped her tea while Zeller sat and digested the information. A few tense seconds passed, Colin digging in to the biscuit barrel Zeller had put in the middle of the table. His munching got right on Janine's nerves, and she kicked his foot under the table.

"What now?" Colin asked.

"Eat quietly, will you?" Janine made eye contact with Zeller. "He also killed Annabel Hawkins."

Zeller nodded. "God." He took a Hobnob out of the barrel. Dipped it in his tea and ate the soggy half before it fell off.

Janine found a custard cream but didn't dunk. "You were on the right track," she said by way of softening things.

Zeller would likely be beating himself up for not spotting that Clarke was a dodgy fucker. Like he hadn't spotted *she* was.

Zeller shrugged. "But I wasn't anywhere near guessing who Peter had paid to do it, and that annoys me."

"But we know now, before…"

"Hmm, before I die. I have that one case I couldn't solve, solved. Yes, there is that, and I'm grateful to you for it. No copper likes retiring with loose ends still dangling."

Zeller and Colin chatted for a while about Colin's future retirement, although Janine's mind wasn't on the conversation. She'd been waiting for her period for a couple of weeks, and it hadn't come. She'd forgotten to take a pill or three since the start of the Slasher business, telling herself it had been in her system for years so she likely wouldn't get caught. This morning, before collecting Colin when the call had come in about Peter, she'd nipped into the chemist and bought a test. When she'd do it, she didn't know. She wasn't sure she wanted to see the truth on a white stick: didn't want to be pleased she was pregnant, because she'd sworn she didn't want kids. Cameron had been right when he'd said little Luke, the abandoned baby from the last big case, had swayed her thinking.

She fucking hated other people proving her wrong.

And she had a dilemma. If the test proved positive, she'd eventually have to go on maternity leave, which meant the twins wouldn't have a copper on hand. She glanced at Colin. No, he'd already expressed his disgust regarding bent coppers, so it wouldn't be any good approaching him to take her place.

So who else would fit the bill?

She'd have to think about it before she let her secret out of the bag.

Chapter Thirty-Six

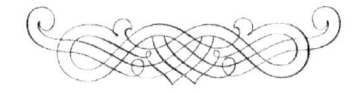

On Boxing Day evening, Katy Marlborough had yet again waylaid Ichabod at Jackpot Palace. He was so sick of her not getting the hint. He thought he'd been blatant about his feelings that night in The Angel, but she'd clearly disregarded what he'd said and was intent on him going out on a date with her whether he liked it or not. How had she become so obsessed with him?

How did ye become so obsessed with Marleigh?

Ichabod was going to have to do it. Go on a date. George and Greg had asked him to get to know Katy. Ever since her sister, Josephine, had been caught up in Pippa's story, they'd been meaning to poke into Katy a bit more. Josephine had run a drug operation from an office with her now-dead lover, Dickie Feathers, and the twins wanted to know if Katy had been aware of that. If she had, they felt she was complicit in what Dickie, Josephine, and their son, Chesney, had been up to. The fact that all three were now dead didn't come into it. Katy might have taken over the business and be selling drugs elsewhere without permission. She'd be allowed if she paid The Brothers protection money, but she didn't.

Ichabod did whatever George and Greg told him, and much as he didn't relish the idea of pretending to like her, he'd do it. He owed them, they'd changed his life, and he felt obliged to be their yes-man.

Katy smiled and touched his arm, her long red fingernails digging in. "I'm a persistent woman, as you'll have realised, and I don't give up easily."

"All right," he said on a sigh. "I'll go on a date wid ye. Ye've ground me down, so ye have."

She let out her irritating, tinkling laugh and kissed him on the cheek, the greasy feel of her scarlet lipstick bugging the shite out of him.

What the feck have I got myself into?

In The Angel, he'd told her he didn't fancy her. Why wasn't she reminding him of that now? Was she so convinced no man could resist her that she refused to contemplate his words?

"When will we go?" she asked. "It'll have to be Up West, of course."

Expensive cow.

"Hmm," he said, scrubbing at his cheeks. He stared over her shoulder as George and Greg waded through the crowd towards him. "Hang on a minute. I have tae see what the bosses want."

He walked away from her, relieved to be out of her presence, and strode to the door that led to the offices. He pushed through into the corridor and waited for the twins to join him.

"What's the story?" he asked.

George put a hand on his shoulder. "We need you to do something else as well as entertaining Katy."

"Aww, what is it?"

"We got a call from Marleigh…"

Ichabod's stomach flipped. Marleigh Jasper, the woman he fancied something rotten but couldn't have. "What's happened?"

"It's David."

Ichabod frowned. "Her husband?"

"Yeah, she's discovered he's been a naughty boy. All those trips abroad? He's a fucking drug trafficker."

That big house. How rich they are. Marleigh being left behind, David saying she couldn't go with him all that often. It makes sense now. "What the feck's it got tae do wid ye? They live on Goldie's old estate."

"Yep, but Moon's taken it over, hasn't he, and he's still away in Amsterdam, so we said we'd help out. You know Marleigh, she trusts you. We're going to set up a sting with her to catch David."

"That's going tae be a big job fer me. Can't I bin Katy until it's sorted?" Ichabod paused. "Feck it, I've already told her I'll go on a date."

George smiled. "Then you'll have to juggle two ladies."

Ichabod sighed. "All right."

"We'll discuss it tomorrow. David's pissed Marleigh off by staying away for Christmas. He's due back the day after tomorrow, so we have time to plan."

Ichabod nodded and followed them out into the casino. Katy had been waiting, and she threw herself at him, her perfume going right up his nose.

As she hugged the life out of him, he thought about David and how devoted Marleigh had been to him. That man didn't deserve how much she loved him.

The darkness that had inhabited Ichabod when he'd lived in Ireland came for a visit, filling him up and spreading until he couldn't breathe.

I'll kill that bastard myself, let alone the twins doin' it. I'll cut his feckin' head off.

To be continued in *Rabbit,*
The Cardigan Estate 26

Printed in Great Britain
by Amazon